FLORIDA NURSE

The daughter of a doctor, Leona Gregory had known since earliest childhood that she wanted to be a nurse. She had always thought that that would mean working with her father. But now that Dr. Gregory had married a young wife, Leona felt out of place in the household. The young RN gratefully accepted a position in a hospital in Cypress City on the Gulf Coast, even though she was afraid it would cut her off from everything she had known. Meeting the cold, beautiful supervisor of nurses, Paula Ingram, and the stern disciplinarian, Dr. Foster, who headed the hospital, seemed to confirm her fears. But Leona also found an opportunity for service she could not have had elsewhere. Then too, there was the handsome, charming senior intern, Cole Jordan . . . and, working with him, Leona began to feel that her heart might find wings again.

PEGGY DERN

FLORIDA NURSE

Complete and Unabridged

LINFORD
Leicester

Originally published as Leona Gregory R.N.

First Linford Edition
published January 1989

British Library CIP Data

Dern, Peggy
  Florida nurse.—Large print ed.—
  Linford romance library
  I. Title
  813′.54[F]

  ISBN 0-7089-6644-6

Published by
F. A. Thorpe (Publishing) Ltd.
Anstey, Leicestershire
Set by Rowland Phototypesetting Ltd.
Bury St. Edmunds, Suffolk
Printed and bound in Great Britain by
T. J. Press (Padstow) Ltd., Padstow, Cornwall

1

LEONA parked the small car in the graveled drive and sat studying the house before her. A solid gray stone house, it was nestled deep in shrubbery that on this chilly February evening was wracked by an icy wind. It was the house where she had been born, where she had grown up, which she had left only to enter the nurses' training school at Blake Memorial. Her one fond dream was to be a very good nurse and to work with her father, Dr. Amos.

It was a long cherished dream. Since her mother's death when she was nine, she had cradled the dream. She and her father, drawn very close by the loss of their cherished companion, had planned it all in long evenings before the fire in the winter. She had gone with him on trips, and they had looked forward to the day when, with her RN pin shining brightly, her chestnut-brown hair crowned by a perky little cap, she would be his aide.

Her mouth twisted now as she studied the house. Somehow it seemed alien and strange to her. And no matter how much she denounced herself for the ugly emotion of jealousy, she knew it was that which was sending her flying south tomorrow to the small hospital on the Gulf Coast of Florida among strangers. For the solid-looking gray house no longer seemed her home. Now Irene was mistress of it. And somehow Leona could not lower the barriers her father's marriage to Irene two years before had erected.

She sighed, grimaced and slid out of the little car. She walked across the drive and put her thumb on the door button and heard the mellow chimes.

The door swung open before her and her father stood there: short, stocky, graying, a pipe clenched between his teeth, and wearing a shabby old smoking

2

jacket she had given him for his birthday years ago.

"Well, come in, come in, child. Or are you auditioning for pneumonia?" Her father reached out a loving hand and urged her into the house. "Did you lose your key? Since when do you have to ring the bell at your own home?"

"Oh, I'm the formal type, I suppose." Leona laughed and kissed her father's cheek and stiffened ever so slightly as she looked beyond him and saw Irene in the doorway of the living room.

For just a moment her eyes met Irene's and held. Irene watched her for a moment, and then she turned away, her shoulders drooping slightly.

"About the key, Dad," Leona made herself say gaily: "now that I'm going away for at least a year, I won't be needing it. I'll leave it at the office for you, and you can pick it up on your next call at the hospital."

Her father drew her into the living room, where Irene smiled a warm

3

greeting, though her lovely eyes were faintly wary.

"Now that's something else I could bear to find out about," said Dr. Amos, as he studied her shrewdly. "What's this about your going away for at least a year?"

Leona smiled faintly as Irene relieved her of her coat, then turned once more to her father.

"Now you know all about that, Dad," she protested lightly. "Dr. Foster wrote you and asked about my qualifications, aside from the fact that I am your daughter."

His father waved his pipe carelessly.

"Oh, sure, I know you've got a job with Dr. Foster at that hospital of his at Cypress City," he agreed. "What I'd like to know is *why* you are leaving Blake Memorial. I thought when you refused to come into the office with me after your graduation it was that you wanted a more varied experience, which you certainly get at Blake Memorial. But now you're kiting off to a little fifty-bed hospital in a half-

4

lost small town. Surely you're not doing that to gain experience?"

Irene said quietly, her tone gentle, "Don't tease the child, Amos dear. After the brutal winter we had, I'm sure she wants to find a warmer climate for a while. I have heard that part of Florida is delightful, in the spring especially."

"Oh, is that it?" asked Dr. Amos innocently. "Now that I can understand. It has been a brutal winter, and you'll enjoy lolling around on the beach and maybe doing a bit of fishing."

"Ha!" Leona's laugh was gay. "Can you imagine an RN in a fifty-bed hospital lolling on the beach? I'll probably be doing my lolling in the o.r. since Dr. Foster was very insistent that he have a nurse with surgical training."

Dr. Amos nodded, his eyes warm and tender. "He's getting one of the best," he said firmly.

"Oh, I bet you say that to all your nurses!" Leona derided him gaily.

"Only to the ones that are my daughters." Dr. Amos grinned.

"Excuse me while I see how Stella is getting along with dinner," said Irene, and went quietly out of the room.

Leona turned a startled face to her father.

"Stella?" she repeated.

"The cook," Dr. Amos explained.

"Well, what happened to Mary-Lou?"

"She quit."

Leona's eyes rounded in astonishment and disbelief.

"After seventeen years working here?" she protested.

"She quit to take care of her daughter's children," Dr. Amos insisted. "Julie, her daughter, was killed by a hit-and-run driver six months ago. Ben, Julie's husband, is a master carpenter and makes a very good income. But there are six children, all under twelve; and the attempts to get a housekeeper to take care of them and run the house were disastrous. So Mary-Lou asked us to let her go and live with them."

"Well, of course," said Leona, feeling a trifle deflated.

"Stella is an old friend of Mary-Lou's and is under strict orders from Mary-Lou to take as good care of us as she always did," Dr. Amos told her.

"And does she?"

"Irene is delighted with her."

Obviously to Dr. Amos there was no higher praise than that. A moment later Irene came back, smiling and gracious and very lovely, to tell them that dinner was ready.

Stella proved to be a tall, powerfully built yellow-skinned woman close to fifty; ample of girth yet not fat. Before the meal was over, Leona knew that Stella was a superlative cook, and that Irene and her father were very lucky to have her.

They were having coffee in the living room when Dr. Amos was summoned to the telephone. He came back, shrugging into his overcoat, and announced an unexpected house call.

"You wait right here until I get back, Baby," he told Leona as he bent to kiss her cheek. "See that she stays, Irene honey."

He kissed Irene with the ardor of a much younger man, and Leona caught the lovely radiance in Irene's eyes and the way her hand clung to his for just a moment before he was gone.

The two women sat in silence with their coffee cups in hand while the sound of Dr. Amos' car died away in the blustery night. It was Irene who broke the silence.

"So you are really going," she said quietly.

"Well, of course, I've signed a year's contract."

"I'm glad," said Irene in that quiet voice that somehow had the ability to ruffle Leona.

"Are you? So am I," she answered through her teeth.

Irene's smile was faint.

"But not for the same reason, I'm sure," she said, and there was a faintly mocking tone in her soft musical voice.

"Well, of course I have no idea why you are glad," Leona began.

"Haven't you? I should think it was very obvious," Irene answered.

8

"I can't think why."

"You've made your father very unhappy, Leona, by refusing to accept me," Irene began. "Oh, I know how close you and he have been since your mother died. And I wanted more than anything else in the world for the three of us to be a family. But you just wouldn't have it that way. You've resented me from the very first moment you knew your father wanted to marry me. And I'm sure you must realize how very selfish that was of you."

Leona bristled indignantly, but before she could speak Irene went on:

"Your father was a very lonely man, Leona, while you were in training. I was lonely, too. I fell in love with my doctor, as a great many feminine patients do; only I was luckier than most. He fell in love with me, too."

"And I couldn't be happier for both of you," Leona said.

"Couldn't you? I wish you could. Believe me, Leona, the only thing that

9

keeps us from being blissfully happy is the fact that you resent me."

"Does that surprise you? It shouldn't."

There was the light of battle in Leona's eyes, and she was honestly relieved that the inevitable moment of plain speaking had finally arrived.

Irene studied her curiously.

"As a matter of fact, it does surprise me quite a bit," she admitted. "If you were a teen-ager and had to live here with us, then I could understand it, perhaps even know how to combat it. But you're grown up. You have your profession, which I know you love. You are free to live anywhere you like," she said slowly.

"Which is why I'm going to Florida," said Leona harshly.

Irene nodded. "Your father wanted very much to have you come into the office and work with him," she pointed out. "He wanted you to live here with us. We would have been so very glad to have you, Leona. But you insist on hating me."

Leona stood up swiftly. Her color had faded, though her eyes still held anger.

"I don't hate you, Irene," she said sharply. "I just feel I'd be better off somewhere else."

"I'm not trying to persuade you to change your mind, Leona," Irene said gently, hurt still visible in her lovely eyes.

"That's good, because I couldn't change my mind now, even if I wanted to. I've signed a contract," Leona told her. "But I wouldn't, anyway, because I don't want to."

Irene nodded.

"I'm sorry, Leona. I really wanted us to be friends, for your father's sake as well as my own. I really admire you very much, Leona."

Caught off balance by the unexpectedness of that, Leona stared at her.

"You admire me?" she repeated incredulously.

"Very much," Irene answered. "Oh, not only because you are young and beautiful and a very fine nurse, although you are all of those. I think I admire you most of all because you've been able to do so many things I once wanted to do and never had the strength of character even to attempt."

Leona stared at her in amazement.

"You wanted to be a nurse?" she asked.

Irene nodded and smiled faintly. "Does that seem so incredible to you? It's quite true. But my family had other plans for me, and I hadn't the strength of character to fight them. So it was the usual silly business for a family like mine: the right schools; the right formal introduction to society; the mad social whirl."

Her tone was bitter, but she made herself smile as she looked up at Leona.

"Unforgivable of me to burden you with the story of my life, I know, and I apologize. But it's the first opportunity we've had to be alone, to talk. So please forgive me. I would like so much for you to understand what Amos means to me. Do you mind?"

Shaken in spite of herself, Leona sat down again and said thinly, "Why, no, of course not. I remember reading about you in the society pages. You made your formal debut in France, didn't you, at Versailles?"

Irene nodded. "Quite a marvelous experience," she drawled, "Or so everyone insisted at the time. Anyway, not long after that I met Tim."

She was silent for a moment, her lovely eyes soft with memories.

"Timothy Jerome Cullman IVth," she mused aloud. "The very picture of any girl's Prince Charming! I was considered the luckiest girl in the world when our engagement was announced. And when we were married, the world seemed to be ours. And there was very little of the world we didn't see during those first few years. I didn't realize until it was too late that Tim was becoming an alcoholic."

Once more her voice dropped into a pit of silence.

"There were miserable years," Irene went on at last, "until Tim was killed in a sordid brawl in a roadside tavern and I went to pieces."

"I remember when that happened. You became a patient of Dad's, and he was terribly worried about you," Leona admitted.

"He brought me back from purgatory," Irene said simply. "He gave me back a sense of decency, of a world that wasn't entirely rotten; he gave me the will to live because he convinced me there was something good for me to live for. And there was: his love and the love I felt for him. Can you understand now, Leona, why there's nothing on earth I wouldn't do for him and why, more than anything, I want to be friends with you; want him to know that we are friends?"

Once more Leona stood up and turned her face away from the plea in Irene's beautiful eyes.

"Oh, I don't think he feels so badly about our not being friends," she said curtly. "And I have accepted you as his wife. I hope you both will be very, very happy for a great many years. And now I'd better go."

Irene made a little weary gesture.

"I haven't gotten through to you at all, have I?" she said, and there was despair and heartache in her voice.

"Look," said Leona swiftly, and hated herself for the sharpness in her voice that she was unable to control, "I'm delighted that you and Dad are so happy. But I am not coming back here to live, and I am not going to work with him in the office, and that's that! I think it will be much better all around if I go down to Cypress City for a year, and then we'll see. And now good night!"

She marched out of the house, and Irene did not rise or make the slightest gesture to stop her.

2

LEONA'S first impression of Cypress City as she drove into it was the golden blaze of sunlight spilling over the small, neat-looking city. She had been driving through warm sunshine for the past two days. But here at Cypress City the sunshine seemed brighter and thicker, as if it could be sliced and spread between bread to make a celestial sandwich.

Her second impression was an equally delightful one. It seemed that nobody was in a hurry! And after the hustle and bustle and clamor of Atlanta, the smoke and grime and exhaust fumes of a myriad motor vehicles, this was like an oasis. Oh, there were cars, of course. She doubted if there was any place in the whole country where there were not cars. But here at least there were not enough of them to pollute the air.

She had been diverted from the main north-south highway some ten miles back; and her way had led along well-paved roads through great groves of citrus trees. She had marveled delightedly at the sight of the trees, row on row of them, as neatly spaced and as arrow-straight in their rows as though they had been planted by surveyors' instruments. And among the dark leaves there were globes of fruit, green, some yellowing, some ripe. And great clusters of blossoms drugged the air with an almost cloying sweetness.

She was delighted by the sight of the first homes. They looked like enormous sugar cubes, cement-block stucco bungalows set neatly in the middle of velvety, emerald-green lawns where lawn sprayers splashed crystal water that made rainbows in the mid-afternoon sunlight. Tall palms were like giant feather dusters that could all but brush the incredibly blue sky that was guiltless of the smallest cloud.

The main street of Cypress City was straight and broad, and there was a planting of palms and flower beds in the center. Such traffic as there was at this time of the mid-afternoon flowed on either side of it. Cars were parked along the curbs, and a few people stirred. Overhead the sun blazed down with a heat that seemed much more suitable for July than for February.

Leona stopped at a service station, and a brisk young man in an immaculate uniform rushed promptly out to the car, smiling a friendly greeting and taking a swift look at her license plates.

"Fill her up, miss?" he suggested hopefully, and beamed when Leona nodded. "Sure glad you stopped by, miss. We don't get many tourists in Cypress City, now that the new highway is finished along the coast."

"Oh, I'm not a tourist." Leona warmed to his friendliness. "I'm going to be working at the Cypress General Hospital. Please tell me how to get there."

"Well, say, that's swell," said the young man. "Straight ahead two miles and you'll see the sign. We're sure proud of our hospital."

"I'm glad to hear that."

"You a nurse?"

"Yes," Leona told him, and handed him her credit card.

"I hope you'll stop in again, Miss Gregory," said the man as she signed the slip he handed her.

"Thanks, I will." Leona smiled at him as she drove out.

The main street, which a sign told her was Orange Avenue, ran straight through the town. There were shops and stores and a couple of three storied-buildings along its three-block length, and then she was once again in a residental district with neat, pretty houses, white or pastel-colored, with lawns and bright splashes of bougainvillea and clumps of poinsettias. Leona slowed her car and her eyes widened as she saw the size and color of them. They were as large as dinner plates, brilliant red, pale pink and creamy white; and some were double-bloomed, looking like enormous rosettes.

I'm going to like it here, she told herself happily as she saw ahead of her the two tall coquina-rock posts that carried a large sign with the name of the hospital. The posts were draped in flame vine, and a few tendrils had climbed up to the sign itself.

She drove up over a shell-strewn drive that crunched beneath the wheels of her car, came to a halt in front of the hospital itself and sat for a moment staring at it. She wondered if, after all, she had made a mistake. This didn't look in the least like a hospital. It looked like an old-fashioned resort hotel!

Leona parked her car in the space at the left of the drive and went up the steps and across the wide verandah. She swung open the screen-door and stepped into a wide, cool lobby.

A pretty dark-skinned girl sat at the switchboard behind a low desk and eyed Leona with friendly curiosity as Leona came over to her.

"I'm Leona Gregory; I wonder if you could tell me where I can find Dr. Foster?"

"Oh yes, Miss Gregory. We've been

expecting you." The girl smiled eagerly. "I'll let Miss Ingram know you are here."

A moment later a woman came down the corridor beyond the wide stairs, and Leona decided she was one of the most beautiful women she had ever seen: tall, regal, her uniform immaculate, her sleekly brushed black hair tucked in a low knot at the back of her neck, a small white cap crowning the shining hair. Her eyes, large and surprisingly blue, swept Leona with a swift, comprehensive glance as she said smoothly, "I'm glad you've finally arrived, Miss Gregory."

"Finally?" Leona repeated, startled. "But I wasn't due to arrive until today."

"We expected you yesterday," said the woman, and there was a faint curtness in her voice. "I'm Paula Ingram, superintendent of nurses. I hope you'll be very happy with us."

Despite the words, the tone of her voice made it an empty phrase. Without waiting for an answer she turned to the girl at the switchboard.

"Ruth, have somebody attend to Miss

Gregory's baggage. If you'll come with me, Miss Gregory, I'll show you to your room."

Once more without waiting for an answer, she turned away and began to mount the wide curving stairs. Just then a man came hurrying out of the same corridor from which she herself had emerged, hastily buttoning on a white coat and pausing as he looked up and saw Miss Ingram watching him sternly.

"What are you doing working in the kitchen, Bart?" Miss Ingram demanded. "Was it necessary?"

"Well, yessum, Miss Ingram. One of the kitchen help didn't show up."

"Charlie Bowlegs, of course."

Bart would not quite meet her eyes.

"Well, yessum, it was Charlie. But he'll be here tomorrow. Seems like there's some sort of tribal doin's, and he had to be there, him being the Chief's son."

"He's probably drunk as usual." Miss Ingram sniffed. "Well, get Miss Gregory's luggage from her car and bring it up to her room."

The man hurried out as though relieved to escape, and Miss Ingram went on up the stairs, speaking over her shoulder to Leona.

"We're here at the edge of the Everglades, and it was a provision of Uncle Dan's will that we give employment to as many of the Seminoles as possible," she explained. "Some of the kitchen help are just a few steps removed from the jungle, though some of the others have gone to school and show some desire to improve themselves. Of course they are poorly paid, which is something we can't help. Our budget is constantly being strained to the breaking point."

By now they had reached the top of the stairs, and Miss Ingram led the way down the corridor toward the back and around an L-shaped angle to a row of doors. She opened one of them and stepped back, motioning Leona to precede her.

The room was quite small, furnished only with a single bed, a white-painted dresser with a mirror and several drawers. The rug was of grass and not new. The closet was a thin, shallow affair. But there were clean, cheerfully patterned chintz curtains at the one window and a matching bedspread and a cushion on the wicker chair beside the window.

"It's not very luxurious, I admit," Miss Ingram told Leona brusquely. "But I'm afraid it's the best we can do; so I hope you can make yourself comfortable."

Before Leona could answer there was a long, low scream; a cry that went up and up and up until suddenly it fell away into shuddering silence. It came from down the main corridor, and as Leona followed Miss Ingram toward it a girl in a uniform that marked her as a nurse's aide came running down the corridor toward Miss Ingram.

"It's Mrs. Blake, Paula. She's gone and her husband is hysterical. Dr. Foster wants you."

"Of course, Alma," Miss Ingram said swiftly, and indicated Leona. "This is Miss Gregory, the new nurse. Will you stay and help her get settled? And, Alma, although you're not a nurse, haven't you been here long enough to know the rules about running in the corridors? A nurse moves swiftly when it's necessary; but she never runs lest she alarm the patients."

"I'm sorry, Paula," Alma began apologetically. But Miss Ingram had moved swiftly away without waiting for an answer, since it was obvious she could not imagine anybody questioning her orders.

The girl stood watching her for a moment, and then she sighed, shrugged and turned back to Leona.

"Well, hi there," she greeted Leona with a warm, friendly smile. "I'm Alma Pruitt. Welcome to the salt mines."

"Leona Gregory and hi yourself." Leona smiled back at her. "Salt mines? That sounds pretty ominous. Come on in while I unpack and tell me about it."

They stood aside while the attendant in the white coat set Leona's bags down and then removed himself.

"Want any help?" asked Alma as Leona picked up the larger of the two bags and placed it on the wooden stand at the foot of the bed.

"No, if you have time just sit down and give me a run-down on what goes on here," suggested Leona. "Miss Ingram is very beautiful, isn't she?"

Alma fished in the pocket of her gray-blue pinafore and brought up a package of cigarettes. As she lit one she chuckled wryly.

"Our Paula beautiful? Well, yes, she is. Only don't ever step a foot out of line or she'll really mow you down. She's a real hard-hearted Hannah, that one."

Leona chuckled. "I have yet to meet a nurse or a nurse's aide who didn't think that about a superintendent of nurses," she said. "It seems to me that's part of their job. To keep all us underlings so scared of them we don't dare step a foot out of line."

"She and Dr. Foster are a fine pair of Gloomy Gusses! They never seem to smile or to have a light-hearted thought," Alma mused aloud as Leona went on briskly unpacking. "Still, Dr. F. is young for all the responsibilities he carries; and he is dedicated to carrying out Uncle Dan's fondest dreams of what Harbor General should be."

"Miss Ingram mentioned an Uncle Dan. Who is he?" asked Leona with not unnatural curiosity.

"Was, not is," Alma told her. "Uncle Dan was a pioneer who came to this section of the country when he was a baby. When he died, three years ago, he was almost a hundred. He built up the whole place. Made friends with the Seminoles; fought to get schools for them; did just about everything he could think of to help them. And in return they just about worshipped him. He built this resort hotel back in the 80's, mainly, people said, so he could give employment to some of the younger and brighter members of the tribes. There are a dozen or more different tribes; and they all live and work together so peacefully that sometimes I wonder if the whole world couldn't take a leaf out of their book of 'togetherness' and find out how to live with each other."

"You have a thought there," Leona

admitted. "So Uncle Dan built a resort hotel, and what happened?"

"Oh, people were just beginning to discover Florida back in the 80's. This part of the west coast was still virtually a wilderness, so guests stayed away in large numbers, and the hotel was closed," Alma rattled on cheerfully. "But Uncle Dan had been a busy little beaver; teaching people that this was grand citrus country and fine cattle country and using the money his folks brought with them to make a lot more money and invest it in more and more land. Dr. F. came here about eight years ago. When Uncle Dan was sick, Dr. Foster took care of him and, like it says in the story-books, a deep friendship sprang up between the two men. Dr. Foster wanted a hospital, and Uncle Dan gave him the cypress City Hotel, and now it's Cypress Harbor General Hospital."

"What a nice story," said Leona. "You'd have thought this Uncle Dan would have wanted the hospital to be named for him as a sort of memorial."

"Not Uncle Dan. He wasn't that type." Alma answered. "My Gramps and Uncle Dan were buddies. Gramps came down here because he had heard about the things Uncle Dan was doing, and the first thing you know they were practically living in each other's pockets, though Uncle Dan called Gramps 'that young whippersnapper' because Gramps was about thirty years younger than Uncle Dan. Between them they just about made this place. Uncle Dan said he wanted the hospital to be a harbor of hope for all the sick and ailing and hurt, regardless of race, creed or color. So it was called Cypress City Harbor Hospital."

"And you work here as a nurse's aide?" asked Leona curiously.

Alma grinned, and there was an impish twinkle in her eyes as she answered demurely. "When Gramps will let me get away from home long enough. He claims I'm needed at the farm."

"Oh, your grandfather has a farm here?" asked Leona.

"Well, yes, I imagine you could call it a farm," said Alma demurely.

Alma was a ravishing brunette, her hair a thick soft mass of cropped black curls, her eyes a warm golden brown. She was sun-tanned to a delicious toast-brown, and her blue-and-white striped pinafore, over a white uniform with a small red and white sleeve insignia, was vastly becoming.

Suddenly Alma's gaiety faded and her red mouth drooped.

"But of course now that Gramps is here in the hospital, he feels even more my place is at the farm," she admitted huskily.

"Oh, is your grandfather on the staff here?" Leona asked.

"Heck, no! He's a patient, and how he hates it, the poor darling," Alma answered. "Phlebitis. And he says for a man his age it's downright disgusting. Dr. Foster is planning an operation. I suppose you know what they call the operation?"

"A phlebotomy?"

Alma nodded soberly. "I think so. Dr. Foster's ordered some of that terribly expensive medicine that's supposed to dissolve the blood clot, but so far it hasn't helped much. At fifty dollars a 'shot', you'd think it would, wouldn't you? I suppose you know all about that, don't you?"

"Alma dear, nobody knows 'all about' any of the so-called miracle drugs or wonder drugs," Leona said quite honestly. "I've served in the operating room for phlebotomies, of course and while they are no fun, they aren't too dangerous."

Alma stood up, and Leona saw that her hands were tightly clenched in the pockets of her pinafore and there was a mist of tears obscuring the warm golden brown of her eyes.

"My Gramps is just about the grandest guy that ever walked in shoe leather." Alma's voice shook despite her efforts to steady it. "And if anything happens to him, I'll just about tear this place down with my bare hands!"

And swiftly, without giving Leona a chance to answer, she turned and ran out of the room.

3

LEONA left her room a little later and walked along the corridor.

She was almost at the head of the stairs when a voice called to her and she turned to see a man coming toward her from the wing opposite that from which she had emerged. She waited, and as he approached she realized that he was enormously good-looking. His hospital whites set off his deep sun-tan, topped by dark red hair. His gray-green eyes were lively with interest and admiration as he reached her.

"Well, hello there!" he greeted her warmly, his voice deep and vibrant and a perfect accompaniment to his spectacular good looks. "You must be the new 'angel without wings' we've been expecting."

Leona laughed. "Well, I'm Leona Gregory, Doctor. But it's been a long time since I've heard myself referred to as 'an angel without wings'."

"It must have been when you were very young, you poor, doddering old thing," he commiserated.

"Why, yes, I think it must have been back when I was a 'candy-striper' and hadn't quite convinced myself I really would ever be an RN," Leona admitted demurely.

"And I bet you were just about the cutest 'candy-striper' that ever wore a peppermint-stick uniform," he commented.

"I can't recall that there were any complaints," Leona admitted.

"I'll just bet there weren't," he told her. "Like to make the rounds with me? I'm Cole Jordan, senior intern, if you're interested."

"Well, of course I'm interested, Dr. Jordan, since we are going to be working together." Leona hesitated, a small frown drawing her brows close. "But shouldn't I make my first round with Dr. Foster, or perhaps Miss Ingram? That was the way we did it back at Blake Memorial."

Dr. Jordan's smile faded slightly.

"A snow, eh?" he mocked her. "You're not only an RN but a well-trained little RN—a stickler for rules and regulations, aren't you?"

Leona answered quietly, all trace of mockery gone from her voice, "I like to get off on the right foot, Dr. Jordan. I wouldn't want to go against any of the rules here."

Dr. Jordan nodded. His eyes were now touched with a reluctant respect.

"And right you are," he told her quietly. "I understand you've signed for a year's tour of duty, and I've got six more months to go. So that should give us a chance to get even better acquainted. I'll be looking forward to it, pretty thing."

He grinned at the tide of color that swept over her face at the words and at his tone of voice. He lifted his hand, gave her an amused salute and went his way.

Leona had reached the halfway point of the stairs when she saw a group in the lobby and paused. Two men and two women were facing a man who stood with his back to her. They were poorly dressed and their faces were strained with anxiety and fear. The man who stood facing them, his back to Leona, was slightly above medium height. His upthrust head was bare, and the sunlight that crept through the window shone on dark hair faintly touched with gray.

"The tumor may or may not be malignant," he was saying as Leona paused on the stairs. "That is something we can't say until we operate and tests are made. But the child must have the operation. There is no doubt about that. I've set the time for eight a.m. tomorrow."

One of the men said belligerently, "We haven't given our permission for you to operate. And you can't unless we're willing."

"No, you have a right to let her die if that's the way you want it," the doctor told the group, and one of the women gave a low, keening wail and hid her face against the other woman's breast.

The man who had spoken said sharply, "You got no right to talk to us like that, Doc. She ain't but five years old. Stands to reason we don't want her cut up 'less it's her only chance."

"And I've told you it is," snapped Dr. Foster.

The man looked uncertainly at the weeping woman.

"If she don't have the operation she'll —she'll—" he could not utter the word.

"She'll die," Dr. Foster helped him out. "She may live a month, even two or three. But there will always be the danger that the tumor is malignant."

"You mean maybe it's cancer?" the man asked, stiff-lipped.

"There's a good chance that it is," Dr. Foster stated brusquely. "There is also the chance that it isn't. But without the operation there is no way of knowing."

The woman was sobbing against the other woman's breast, and the man who was obviously the child's father touched his dry lips with his tongue.

"If she has the operation she'll get well?" he asked huskily.

"There's a fifty-fifty chance, if the tumor is not malignant."

"A fifty-fifty chance?" The man's eyes blazed with fury and his powerful hands knotted into huge sets. "You mean you want to cut her up, and you ain't givin' her no more'n a fifty-fifty chance?"

Dr. Foster's hands were jammed tightly into the pockets of his white coat, and his back was so rigid that Leona realized that he was very angry.

"I can guarantee nothing except that when the operation is over and we run the tests, we'll know whether or not the tumor is malignant," he said harshly.

The man looked at his wife and at his friend, and then he turned once more to Dr. Foster with a pleading look in his eyes. "We got to think this over, Doc. We can't make no decision like that without doing some thinking about it."

"There are three operations scheduled for tomorrow, and your daughter's is the first," Dr. Foster told him sternly.

"There are preparations that must be made tonight if she is to have surgery in the morning. And if she misses her appointment I have no idea how soon we can give her another. We haven't time here for a lot of shilly-shallying. Now do we operate on your daughter at eight in the morning, or do you prefer to take her home with you tonight?"

Until now Leona had not been aware of Paula Ingram standing off to one side of the group. Suddenly, as though she had sensed Leona's presence, Paula looked at her, saw the shock on her face and came swiftly to her.

"Come into my office, Leona," she said swiftly, and drew Leona with her across the lobby and into the small, airy office. "I suppose you think Dr. Foster is being very brusque and very inhuman."

Unwilling to lie, Leona said huskily, "Well, I can't help feeling he might have been a little more understanding and gentle."

Paula smothered a sigh as she dropped

into the chair behind her desk and motioned Leona to one across from it.

"You must not get the wrong impression of Dr. Foster, Leona," she began. "I've worked with him for years. I know him to be a thoroughly competent, well-qualified man; a brilliant surgeon, a dedicated physician and a fine administrator. He simply has not the patience or the time to put up with stupid people who are unwilling for their families to be given the very best service he and the hospital can perform."

Leona said with a trace of spirit, "I wasn't criticizing him, Miss Ingram."

Paula's blue eyes were cold and her voice was tight as she said, "I wouldn't advise you to. You'll be serving under his authority and your first duty will be to trust him implicitly, to obey his orders without question."

"Naturally I expected to do that, Miss Ingram. It's one of the first things I learned when I entered training. It's just that those people were so upset, so distressed, I felt sorry for them."

"They are ignorant, stupid creatures from a fishing village."

"But they're people, human beings."

Paula studied her with a curious intentness, and then she nodded as though she had reached some decision.

"Back in the hospital where you trained, Leona, I'm sure there were enough doctors and interns to sit down and very gently break bad news to the families of patients; to coax them gently and deftly to permit autopsies; to allow operations. Here at the Harbor we have four interns, one senior intern and Dr. Foster. We have four RN's and six PN's, not one of whom is trained for anything but the simplest care of patients. So can't you see that we have to be brief, even brutal, if you want to call if that. There simply isn't time for any of us to sit down and hold the families' hands and soothe them. Our senior intern Cole Jordan, would have taken an hour or more to break the news to those people of the necessity of the child's operation. And his other work would suffer. Dr. Foster

41

simply does not have the time *or* the patience for such nonsense. Either they agree to the operation or they take the child home. We can use the bed she's occupying. There's never room enough here for all the people who need us."

Paula stood up to indicate that the interview was ended. Leona rose, and for a moment the two women looked at each other steadily. And just as Leona had known that she and Alma Pruitt were going to be friends, she knew now that she and Paula Ingram never could be.

Paula said quietly, "There is one more thing, Leona, something I'd like you always to remember, because it will make your stay here much more satisfactory for all concerned."

Leona waited politely, and after a moment Paula's head went up.

"You may dislike Dr. Foster and me as much as you wish," she said icily. "Personally, I prefer that the nurses under me dislike me, because it makes discipline easier. And I grant you that until you get to know Dr. Foster better, you may not find him an easy man to like. I don't think he cares a hoot whether people like him or not. But you must respect his skill and his ability. You must never forget that he is a dedicated surgeon; that his diagnoses are swift, but able and skillful. He never makes a mistake."

"Never, Miss Ingram?" The words slipped from Leona's tongue, even though she knew they were ill-advised.

"Never, Leona," Paula insisted harshly, her eyes blazing. "Don't forget that, ever."

"No, Miss Ingram." Leona's words came through her teeth, emptily polite, quite free of any significance or warmth.

"Good! See that you don't." Paula was stiff and unbending. "I know you aren't supposed to go on duty until morning, but since you are in uniform, I'd appreciate it if you would relieve Jane Lester in the charity ward for an hour or so. She's doing double duty today because one of the PN's is away for the day."

"I'll be glad to help in any way I can," said Leona politely.

"Then come along," said Paula, and led the way out of the office.

In the lobby, the group of people had gone and Dr. Foster was just vanishing into his office when Paula called to him. And though she merely said, "Dr. Foster, do you have a minute?" her voice was warm and sweet.

Dr. Foster turned, the angry scowl still on his lean brown face.

"Of course, Paula, What is it?"

"This is Leona Gregory, the new nurse we've been expecting," said Paula. "Since she will be on duty with you in the o.r., I thought she would like to meet you now."

Dr. Foster's eyes swept Leona in a single comprehensive glance.

"Oh, yes, Dr. Gregory's daughter. A very fine man," he said curtly.

"Thank you, Doctor. I think so," Leona responded.

Dr. Foster nodded to her and to Paula and went into his office and closed the door. For a moment Paula stood watching the closed door, and then she drew a long breath and turned to Leona.

"This way, Leona," she said, and led the way down the corridor and to a door behind the stairs that opened into the left wing.

The large room was fitted as a ward. Beds faced each other in a double row the full length of the room, and there was barely room between the beds for small stands on which Medications were placed. The aisles between the double row was wide enough for two or three people to walk abreast.

All of the beds were occupied, and at the far end Leona saw a group of people surrounding Dr. Cole Jordan beside a bed. Her second glance identified the group as the one she had seen talking to Dr. Foster earlier. The group was listening to Dr. Jordan with intense interest. Leona saw that his smile was warm and comforting and knew by the way his fingers touched the small child as he explained what was to be done that his own interest in the problem was keen.

Paula glanced at the group, and her mouth thinned slightly as she walked with her sure, authoritative stride to the desk at the end of the room, facing the ward. A nurse sat behind the desk; as she saw Paula she got swiftly to her feet with a faint trace of apprehension.

"Jane, this is Leona Gregory, the new nurse we've been expecting." Paula made the introduction curtly. "Leona, this is Jane Lester, one of our very best nurses. She's wasted here in the charity ward, but after all, we are painfully understaffed."

Jane, a plain, plump woman in her early thirties, with sandy hair and freckles, smiled shyly at Leona, and Paula made a slight gesture of her head in the direction of Dr. Jordan and the group surrounding him.

"I suppose he's persuading them to permit the operation," she murmured dryly.

"They came to get the little girl, Miss Ingram, and while I was getting the release papers ready for them to sign, Dr. Jordan came in and asked them to reconsider. He took them down to the little girl and began explaining what Dr. Foster planned to do," Jane answered.

"I see," said Paula noncommittally. "I'll leave Leona here with you, Jane, until feeding time. She can help you with the patient's trays and then relieve you so that you can have your own dinner. Dr. Foster will probably want her assigned to surgery as soon as she has had time to familiarize herself with the way we do things here."

She turned and walked away. Leona saw Jane's eyes watching as the swinging door closed behind the tall, hurrying form. Then Jane turned to Leona and grinned ruefully.

"She scares me simple," she admitted in a burst of low-voiced confidence. "Oh, she's a fine nurse and all that. But, boy is she ever strict!"

"Aren't superintendents of nurses supposed to be? I've never met one that wasn't. They scare me, too," Leona confessed.

The group beside the child's bed was

going up the aisle between the double row of beds. The mother moved back to kiss the child and fondle the small, pinched face before she rejoined the others, a handkerchief pressed to her face.

Dr. Jordan guided the group back to Jane's desk and said with a smile, "Mr. and Mrs. Jenkins have decided to allow the operation, Nurse. So we won't be needing those release forms."

"I'm glad, Dr. Jordan," said Jane, and turned with a warm, friendly smile toward the child's parents. "Try not to worry too much about her. Dr. Foster is a very fine surgeon and he'll take good care of her."

"*Him!*" snorted the child's father, and jerked a work-worn thumb toward Dr. Jordan. "Here's the fellow I wish was operating on my little girl. This fellow's still got a little of the milk o' kindness left in him."

Dr. Jordan dropped a friendly hand on the man's shoulder and said pleasantly, "Oh, Dr. Foster is a much better surgeon than I am, Jenkins. He's had much more experience in surgery."

"Maybe he's a better surgeon, though I doubt it; but he ain't no better man than you are, Doc. You'll kind o' stand by and see he don't hurt my little girl?"

"Of course I will, Jenkins," Dr. Jordan said gently. "You go home and get a good night's sleep, both of you. And don't worry any more than you can help. Your little Brenda will be in good hands. I promise you."

He guided them to the door and out, and as the door swung shut behind them, Jane sighed.

"That's our Dr. Cole," she murmured. "He can charm the birdies off the trees when he sets about it. Man, what a 'luxury doc' he's going to be!"

"A 'luxury doc'?" Leona repeated.

"Oh, sure," Jane answered carelessly. "He'd be wasted in a place like this. He belongs where the patients are well-heeled and duly susceptible to his charm, and that's where he's going as soon as he finishes here. I'd like to go with him as his office nurse, but he'll choose one who is a dazzling beauty to match the decor of his magnificently appointed offices."

The swinging doors opened and two pretty girls in red and white striped pinafores, flushed and bright-eyed, pushed in a big double-decker cart on which the supper trays for the patients were set in neat array.

"Hi, Miss Lester," the blonde one greeted her. And the other added youthfully, "Boy, have we been on the jump since we got here. Hope we aren't late."

Jane smiled at them.

"I'd say, judging from the looks of the patients, you're right on time," she assured them, and indicated Leona. "This is Miss Gregory, a new nurse we've just been lucky enough to snare."

"Hello, Miss Gregory," chorused the two girls, beaming, and went about their job of serving the trays.

Leona watched them as they moved down the double row of beds, solicitous for the comfort of the patients. Men, women and two or three children turned eager faces to them as the girls went down the row, laughing, chattering, seeming to fill the whole big ward with their own lovely brand of good cheer.

"Look at them!" said Jane fondly, and there was a touch of maternal pride in her voice. "Aren't they wonderful? And when I think it took us two years to persuade Dr. Foster to accept 'candy-stripers', I can't help marveling."

"Do you suppose you and I were ever that young?" Leona murmured as she saw the pretty brunette bend over a very old woman whose face was as yellow-seamed as parchment and who could hardly open her toothless mouth to receive the food the girl was so carefully spooning.

"You can't be too far from that age yourself," Jane mourned. "Me, I'm so far past it I've forgotten what it was like."

"Were you ever a 'candy-striper'?" asked Leona, watching the two girls.

"Nope. Were you?" asked Jane curiously.

Leona nodded and smiled at the memories her words brought back.

"For three of the happiest years of my life," she answered.

"Oh, and was that when you decided you wanted to be a nurse?"

"Oh, no, I can't remember when I first began to want to be a nurse," Leona answered. "I don't think there was ever any doubt about what I wanted to be. My father is a very fine doctor, and after my mother died, he brought me up. I suppose it just didn't seem possible for me to want to do anything else but to work with him."

For a moment the bitterness of memory thinned her mouth, but Jane seemed not to notice it. She was watching the "candy-stripers".

"I know what you mean," she said soberly. "My mother and father always wanted me to be a nurse. Dad felt it was a noble profession for a woman; that if she had to earn her own living she would be doing something fine and splendid. They always expected me to be the very best nurse anywhere; and bless them, they think I am. They're indecently

52

proud of me. I'd like to take you to visit them some day if by a miracle we can both get the day off together. They operate a fishing camp down in the Everglades. And the Glades are simply fabulous. Uncle Dan would be so happy if he could know that the Glades is now a National Park."

"Oh yes, Alma Pruitt was telling me about Uncle Dan," said Leona.

"Oh, you've met Alma?"

Leona nodded. "She said her family owned a farm near here."

Jane stared at her, her eyebrows raised in amused surprise.

"A *farm?*" she repeated.

Puzzled, Leona asked, "Well, isn't it a farm?"

Jane chuckled. "Well, if you want to call several thousand acres of highly productive citrus, sugar cane and cattle a farm, I suppose you could. Palmadora has its own citrus packing sheds, and the cattle ranch is managed and supervised by a team of expert agricultural graduates."

"My goodness!" Leona was wide-eyed.

"Alma sounded as though it were just a few acres. I suppose that means the family is very rich?"

"Stinkin'," Jane assured her. "There is no family, really, just Mr. Lamar and Alma. He's a patient here. Have you met him? He's a livin' doll, even if he is seventy and sometimes sharp-tongued. There is just one thing in the world Mr. Lamar adores; and that's Alma. And she is equally devoted to him. Next to one another, Palmadora Ranch is their dearest possession. I sometimes think it possesses them instead of the other way around."

"I like her," Leona admitted.

"Everybody does," Jane answered. "Everybody, that is, but Carol Decker, who doesn't like anybody and goes around feeling so sorry for herself that she makes you want to smack her."

Leona asked curiously, "And who, for goodness sake, is Carol Decker?"

"Oh, her mother was Uncle Dan's housekeeper. She came to live at the ranch when Carol was just a baby. Uncle Dan never married, and Carol grew up on the ranch and took it for granted that she and her mother would inherit his entire estate. When he died a couple of years ago and the will was filed for probate, imagine Carol's unbridled fury when she found that a trust fund had been set up for herself and her mother but that the estate had been left to a niece, or any of her living descendents. It took the lawyers several months to locate the heir, and when they did, and he arrived to take over, Carol took one look at him and decided that if she couldn't inherit the estate, maybe she could marry it. And ever since then people have been making bets on whether Bruce MacClain, the nephew, will be able to escape her. She's not what you'd call exactly subtle in her pursuit of him, you see."

The "candy-stripers" had finished and were gathering up the trays. Jane looked on Leona, abashed.

"How I do run on," she mocked herself ruefully. "You must think I'm the world's worst gossip. And you could be so right."

"I don't think so at all," Leona

protested. "I'm glad to know all I can about the place and its people. And I do hope you'll take me to call on your parents. I'd love to see the Everglades. After all, I'll probably never set eyes on the Deckers unless they enter the hospital as patients."

"Which, unless Carol starts behaving herself and stops being such a spiteful, malicious cat, isn't at all unlikely," Jane said darkly. "I doubt if there's a girl in the whole area who is more thoroughly disliked. Sooner or later somebody's going to clobber her. You've heard of people who carry a chip on the shoulder? Carol's is a two-by-four."

The "candy-stripers" had reached the desk now, paused and grinned at Jane.

"Thanks a million, chicks," said Jane. "I don't know what we'd do without your help."

The two girls flushed with pleasure at the praise.

"Oh, we'd like to do a lot more, Miss Lester, if they'd just let us," the blonde said.

"Like help in the operating room," said the brunette wistfully.

There was a twinkle in Jane's eyes.

"Believe me, Lucille, that you wouldn't like, not even when Dr. Cole is there," she said lightly.

Both girls flushed and giggled, and the blonde, wide-eyed, said with limpid innocence, "Why, Miss Lester, I don't know what you mean!"

"Like fun you don't," Jane derided them. "Scoot now, kids. They'll be ready with the trays for the patients upstairs."

"See you tomorrow, Miss Lester," chorused the two girls as they pushed the cart out through the swinging doors.

"That Cole Jordan!" Jane chuckled. "They're all mad about him; not just kids like those, but some of the patients. And don't think he doesn't know it and trade on it. Oh, don't get me wrong, Leona. I like the guy. I admire his ability and his dedication to the profession. And he *is* dedicated. Otherwise he'd never put up with what he has to endure from Dr. F. That one can be really tough when something goes against his grain. And many things do."

She broke off, grimaced at her gossiping and threw a swift glance about the ward.

"All right if I dash along now and feed?" she asked.

"Well, of course," Leona answered. "I feel sure I can cope with whatever happens while you're gone."

"Not much is likely to," Jane comforted her. "And I'll be right back."

"Take your time. I'll study the charts while you are gone." Leona smiled.

"With special attention to the one for Brenda Jenkins, the youngster scheduled for surgery in the morning. I doubt if you'll be assisting as surgical nurse, since you haven't been here long enough to be familiar with our o.r. routine, but Dr. F. may want you to stand by."

Leona nodded and reached for the charts as the swinging door shut behind Jane.

4

WHEN Jane came back Leona was still absorbed in the charts, and Jane grinned cheerfully at her as she urged her to her feet.

"If you're going to be on duty in the o.r. in the morning you'd better scamper along and have supper and get to bed early," she counseled. "And do have a good supper; that is, if you like fish and canned peaches. I once heard somebody say, 'nothing is so inevitable as mashed potatoes on a plate lunch.' I'd amend that to: 'nothing is as inevitable as canned peaches in a hospital dining room'."

"Well, I'm more accustomed to canned peaches than to baked Alaska, and I really like them," Leona said as she went out of the ward and along the corridor.

Just before she reached the dining room door Dr. Jordan strode out of Dr. Foster's office, his handsome face dark

59

with anger, his eyes blazing. He almost ran into Leona before he saw her, pulled himself to a halt and stared down at her.

"Oh, hello there," he greeted her, and slipped a hand beneath her elbow and marched her into the dining room with a force that would not be denied.

"Now wait a minute, Doctor," Leona protested a trifle breathlessly, but he would not listen.

He marched her to a table for two near an open window, yanked a chair back and with a none too gentle hand practically thrust her into it. He walked around to his own chair, seated himself and glared at her.

Leona glared back, her head up, her eyes cold.

"Are you always this impetuous, Dr. Jordan?" she asked coolly.

He looked at her as though he hadn't the faintest idea what she was talking about. And then suddenly he grinned wryly.

"Was I being impetuous?" he offered tacit apology. "Sorry. Guess I was just too blindly angry to realize what I was doing. If you'd rather have your supper alone, just say the word. Of course if you do, I won't budge or allow you to. But you will have stated your wish in the matter, if that's any comfort to you."

A slim, copper-skinned girl in a crisp blue uniform beneath a white apron came swiftly to their table, and Dr. Jordan looked up at her, scowling.

"Wait a minute, don't tell me. Let me guess. It's fish tonight," he said with the air of one making a monumental discovery.

The girl's dark brown eyes twinkled.

"Why, Dr. Jordan, how did you guess?" she asked in her soft, musical voice.

"Oh, I happened to glance at the calendar and saw that it was Friday and knew it would be fish for supper. Perhaps I'm psychic."

"I could make you an omelet, Dr. Jordan," said the girl.

Gratefully, Dr. Jordan asked, *"Would* you?"

"Of course, Dr. Jordan. I'll be glad to."

"It won't create any upheaval in the kitchen?" he asked cautiously.

The girl laughed softly. "Not when I tell them it's for you."

She looked down at Leona and asked, "Would you like an omelet, too, miss?"

"Thanks, I'll have the fish."

The girl turned and went away.

Leona glanced across at Dr. Jordan and said demurely, "You really rate around here, don't you, Doctor?"

"With the hired help, especially in the kitchen," he agreed wryly. "Their chief is a good friend of mine. I took out his appendix when their own medicine man was quite sure their gods wanted him in their Happy Hunting Grounds."

"Oh, is she a Seminole?" asked Leona.

"Of course, didn't you know?" Dr. Jordan was surprised at her question. "Practically all the personnel, except the nurses, interns and the head nurse, Miss Ingram, are Seminoles. Two of the practical nurses are members of Chief

Osceola's tribe. It was a condition of the granting of the hospital to Dr. Foster that he give jobs to as many qualified Seminoles as possible and they held him in as high esteem as any of their own tribal chiefs, even Osceola the greatly revered."

The waitress came back and placed their food before them. Dr. Jordan's omelet was fluffy, done to a turn, and the thick slab of fish on Leona's plate was delicately browned and appetizing.

Leona dug a fork into it, tasted it and looked at Dr. Jordan.

"It's delicious! You're being cheated, Doctor, eating eggs, when you could have something like this. It's delectable. I've ever tasted such fish."

"That's because you've never had it as fresh as that before," he pointed out. "A few hours ago that fish was swimming happily in a nice cool sea, minding his own business, bothering nobody. And then along comes a man with a fishing net—"

"Hush!" pleaded Leona. "You're making me feel sorry for him."

Dr. Jordan chuckled. "Well, then just forget it wasn't bought in a fish market after being shipped halfway across the country in a refigerated truck. Just look on him as something good to eat and enjoy him."

"I will," Leona assured him, "if you'll stop calling it 'him' and reminding me that maybe he has a family that's waiting for him under a rock somewhere."

Dr. Jordan laughed, and his eyes quickened with interest.

"You're a very compassionate person, aren't you?"

"I'm a nurse," she reminded him as though no other answer were required.

"You can feel sorry for people and are still not afraid of getting emotionally involved with their problems?"

"Well, of course that's part of what we were taught in training," she admitted. "But somehow I can't help feeling that being emotionally involved with people is a part of the price we pay for belonging to the human race."

Dr. Jordan was eying her with curiously alert interest.

"Very well put, my girl," he said at last, and his jaw hardened. "Then you aren't going to like it here a little bit. Such human feelings are frowned on by the higher-ups. They much prefer that you be a competent, hard-working underpaid machine without human emotions at all."

"Do they?" asked Leona uneasily.

"They do indeed," he assured her grimly. "Oh, I grant you that we don't have a large enough staff to sit down and go gently and painstakingly over every patient's problems with him. Yet I feel that's part of a doctor's responsibility. How are you going to know what's really wrong with a patient unless you know something about the patient himself, let him talk, give him time to get things off his chest? First thing you know he'll tell you something that will give you at least an inkling as to his real trouble, and chances are that it may be something entirely different from what you first thought. I feel the only really safe diagnosis *must* follow a discussion with the patient, with his family."

He broke off suddenly and gave her a faintly rueful smile.

"I'm beginning to sound like a third-rate psychiatrist," he apologized.

Leona shook her head, her eyes warm and friendly.

"You sound like a man who could easily be a first-rate psychiatrist," she told him gravely. "And I couldn't agree with you more."

"Thanks," said Dr. Jordan, obviously relieved. "You're a very nice child. But surgery is my field. That's why I was glad to do my senior internship here under Dr. Foster. He's really one of the best in his field and a very brilliant man. I'm learning a lot working under him."

"Well, psychiatry is a very valuable part of the entire medical profession, and I'd think it would be especially valuable in surgery," Leona pointed out.

"Well, of course," he agreed, and seemed to realize he had been more than a trifle indiscreet. "See here, I don't know why I'm running on like this."

"Probably because you know how interested I am," Leona pointed out.

He laughed. "That sounds like a well-learned lesson from a famous charm school," he accused her.

"It isn't at all; I'm quite sincere," Leona told him, and added, "You sound like a man who is pretty wary of women and distrusts them all."

"Oh, I wouldn't say that," he countered cautiously. "They're a fascinating sex, but being a doctor makes a man a trifle wary of some of their most intriguing wiles. No charm school?"

Leona laughed and shook her head.

"Nary a charm school!"

He reached across the table and took up her hand.

"No engagement ring?" he asked.

"Nary a one!"

"There must have been a most unenterprising crowd of fellows back there where you trained," he suggested.

"Or it could be that I'm a bit choosy perhaps?" Leona mocked him.

"Well, you won't have the chance to be choosy here," Dr. Jordan assured her. "There are only three unattached males on the staff: Dr. Foster, a junior intern and a fellow named Cole Jordan who's a senior intern in surgery."

"Are you trying to frighten me, Doctor?" she mocked. "I'm not a husband hunter. I'm a nurse. Remember?"

"Sure you are, and a very good one, I'm sure," he agreed cheerfully. "I felt it only fair to warn you about conditions as they exist in these hallowed halls, in case you *did* have a spot of husband hunting in mind."

"You're very kind, Doctor, but I haven't."

The waitress came, bringing dessert, and as she placed the dish in front of Dr. Jordan he looked up at her in wide-eyed surprise.

"Canned pears instead of peaches!

Naomi, you're pampering us," he marvelled.

The girl smiled warmly at him.

"The peaches were all gone, Doctor. The pears had been opened for some of the patient's trays, and I thought you'd like them," she told him.

"You knew I would, and thanks a lot, Naomi," said Dr. Jordan, and indicated Leona. "This is Miss Gregory, who's come to work with us. I'm sure having canned pears for dessert her first night here instead of the traditional peaches will give her a good impression of us."

Naomi smiled shyly at Leona. "I hope so, Miss Gregory."

"The fish did that, Naomi. I never ate anything so delicious," Leona assured her, and the girl smiled and went away.

5

THE following morning found Leona in the operating room, scrubbed, sterile and ready for what might be asked of her. Since Paula was the nurse assisting, Leona was merely required to act as a circulating nurse.

The first patient in the o.r. was the little Jenkins girl. As Dr. Foster's scalpel moved deftly, making the briefest possible incision, removing the small but deadly-looking tumour, Leona felt a moment of dread. *Was* it malignant? And if so, had its deadly tentacles stretched through the child's throat, that small, sunburned throat that looked so vulnerable, so defenseless?

She received the deadly-looking thing, hurried it to the lab for analysis and was back immediately. When the operation was finished and the incision closed, the child trundled on her way to the recovery room, Leona could not keep back a little word of delighted commendation.

She flushed to the roots of her hair when Dr. Foster looked up and glared at her as though Leona had committed blasphemy.

"Brilliant, Nurse?" Dr. Foster repeated her word and made it sound like an epithet. "Why so surprised? Did you think we were butchers here at Harbor Memorial?"

Before Leona could offer the apology both he and Paula seemed to expect, the next operative patient was on the table and the whole staff was once more intent on the task before them. But as he lowered his head above the patient, Dr. Jordan's eyes twinkled at Leona and she thought he gave her the ghost of a comforting wink.

After the third operation of the morning, when the patient had been wheeled away to the recovery room, Leona approached Dr. Foster and, with her head up, said quietly, "I'm very sorry if I seemed presumptuous, Dr. Foster. I truly didn't mean to. But I had become interested in the child and I couldn't help admiring the way you took out that tumor."

Dr. Foster had dragged off his mask but still wore his cap and his pale green gown. He was frowning and his eyes were quite cold.

"Thanks," he said curtly. "I suppose back at Blake Memorial you have enough o.r. teams to make it possible to indulge in a bit of a let-down after a rather tough job?"

"Well, yes, we do," Leona admitted, and felt that he was accusing her of some crime.

"We don't, here," said Dr. Foster curtly. "You'll familiarize yourself with the o.r. and be prepared take Miss Ingram's place at the surgery scheduled for tomorrow."

He turned and strode toward the scrub room, and Leona drew a deep breath as she followed Paula into the nurses' quarters.

Paula removed her cap and gown,

dropped them into the sterilizer and eyed Leona with a look that could hardly be construed as friendly.

"So now you think Dr. Foster is brilliant, do you?" she mocked.

"I never doubted it, Miss Ingram," Leona protested.

"Well, don't! He's wasted here; he belongs somewhere like John Hopkins, where he could be properly appreciated for the brilliant man he is. But he's so loyal to Uncle Dan's memory that he wouldn't leave here even if they offered him the world with a gold crown."

Leona caught the faint trace of bitterness in Paula's voice as she changed into a fresh uniform.

"But he *is* badly needed here, Miss Ingram," Leona ventured.

"Oh, yes, he's badly needed." Paula's lovely mouth twisted as she adjusted the crisp cap to her shining blue-black hair. "But any accredited hack could do what he does here. He belongs where he can accomplish the big things of which he's capable."

"Miss Ingram, I think you're wrong about Dr. Foster," Leona said impulsively. Then as Paula turned sharply on her, eyes angry, she went on swiftly, "I mean about any accredited hack doing the job Dr. Foster does. That tendon transplant this morning was a fine job, and so was that bowel resection. Only a man skilled and competent and very capable could have done such beautiful jobs."

Paula drew a deep, hard breath.

"Oh, he's brilliant and he does fine work and I admit that he is tops in his field," she said. "But I still feel a man of his capabilities is wasted in a tiny place like this."

She glanced at Leona but seemed scarcely conscious of the girl's presence.

"He wants to study the technique for open heart surgery, poor dear," Paula said softly. "It fascinates him. But what chance has he to get away from here long enough to go north and get the necessary training? And what chance have we to get the equipment and the teams trained to handle it? So we have no recourse but to

74

ship our open-heart patients away up north to hospitals which are better equipped and more adequately staffed."

She stood in bitter silence for a moment, and then she seemed to become aware of Leona and dismissed her brusquely.

Leona went out of the room and along the corridor.

As she reached the head of the stairs, Alma Pruitt came up, carefully steadying a laden tray. As she saw Leona, her pretty face lit up with a warm smile.

"Hi there! Come on and meet Gramps," she suggested. "I've been telling him about you. You'll love him; and he'll be crazy about you. Seventy odd he may be, but he still has an eye for a pretty girl!"

Leona laughed and walked beside her to a door at the front of the building. She held it open while Alma went ahead of her, carrying the tray.

The man who lay in bed, propped against pillows, still retained his leathery tan. His thick shock of white hair was rumpled and his eyes were sick with pain. But as Alma came into the room he grinned at her and said with an attempt at bluffness, "Well, it's about time you were getting around here with some vittles. A man could lie here and starve to death while you go skallyhooting around the country."

"Ha!" snapped Alma, and Leona was touched at the girl's valiant attempt at gaiety as they arranged the tray so that the old man could feed himself. "A heck of a lot of skallyhooting *I* get to do, while you're piled up here taking a rest cure! The ranch is going to rack and ruin, and all you do is lie here and stuff yourself!"

The old man looked down at the food on his tray, and his thin lips curled.

"A man would have to be a danged fool to eat this swill," he barked, and looked beyond her to where Leona stood at the foot of the bed, examining his chart. "Who're you?"

"Oh, I forgot," Alma said cheerfully. "Gramps, this is Leona Gregory, and if you behave yourself we just might possibly let her be your special duty nurse. Leona, this outrageous old creature is my Gramps, Lamar Pruitt."

Leona laughed. "Why, thank you, Mr. Pruitt. But Alma is by far the prettiest—"

"Sh. The gal's conceited enough already! Mustn't give her any more fuel to stoke the fires," warned Lamar. "Well, well, so you're going to be my special nurse. I feel a bad relapse coming on. I may be here for months."

"You just dare!" Alma threatened him darkly. "You think I intend to go on doing your job and mine, too?, as you knew darned well I'd have to when you 'chickened out' and sneaked off here to enjoy bad health!"

Lamar chuckled. "I'm smart," he assured her. "How're things going?"

Alma tilted her chin defiantly. "Just dandy, now that you aren't there to keep on throwing monkey wrenches," she told him derisively. "Matter of fact, you just stay right here until we're through picking and shipping fruit and have the cattle ready for auction and the horses are trained to run faster than any others on the track. We'll get along just fine as long as you stay here. I suppose you think you're the indispensable man, huh?"

She caught her breath. Suddenly her gaiety vanished and tears slid down her face as she knelt beside the bed and put her arms about him.

"Oh, Gramps, please hurry up and get well and come on home," she begged. "It's just awful out there without you; so lonely I feel like throwing myself into the lake. If it was deep enough I probably would."

The old man's hand stroked the girl's hair.

"So you miss your old Gramps, do you, baby?" he asked tenderly, his voice a caress.

"Well, of course I do," Alma spluttered, and stood up, fighting to steady herself, to gain her self-control, "like I'd miss an aching tooth after it was out. You hurry out of that bed and come on home, you hear me?"

The old man smiled tenderly at her

78

where she stood above him in a threatening attitude.

"I will, baby, I will," he promised her. "Now you run along and take care of yourself, and I'll be home before you know it."

"Well, you better had, or I'll sue the hospital," Alma said firmly. "I'm tired of doing your work and mine both. Now you hustle out of that bed and get home fast!"

"Yessum," said Lamar meekly, as Alma bent swiftly and kissed his cheek.

Leona followed her from the room and the door closed after them. Alma drew a long shuddering breath and was suddenly weeping in Leona's comforting arms.

"Oh, he looks so awful!" she wailed softly. "He's going to get well, isn't he, Leona?"

"Of course he is. Surgery is scheduled for Thursday, and he's going to be fine. You mustn't worry about him."

"Oh, don't be a fool!" snapped the mercurial Alma hotly. "Not worry about him? Don't you understand? He's all I've got! He's my family. We're a team. I'm

79

never going to marry until I find some-body just exactly like Gramps; and they don't make 'em like that any more. You take good care of him, you hear me?"

"I promise, Miss Pruitt."

"Miss Pruitt my eye," said Alma huskily. "Nobody calls me Miss Pruitt. I'm Alma."

"And I'm Leona, and between us we'll have your grandfather out of here and on his feet and completely recovered before you can say Jack Robinson," Leona promised. She saw Dr. Jordan coming down the corridor. "Here's Dr. Jordan. Do you want to talk to him?"

Alma blew her nose vigorously, mopped her eyes and said ungraciously, "Why should I?"

"Well, he'll be assisting at the oper-ation, and I thought you might want to see what he thinks," Leona pointed out.

"It's Dr. Foster I'm holding account-able," said Alma. And then to Dr. Jordan, "Hello, Cole."

"Alma, love," said Dr. Jordan, "what do you hear from Tampa these days?"

"Oh, I'm wearing him down," said Alma matter of factly. "I'm trying to convince him that I desperately need his help, now that Gramps is laid up. But he won't believe me. He thinks it's a feminine wile to persuade him to forget his cherished principles."

"Your fiancé could be a very smart guy at that," Dr. Jordan said cautiously. "Want me to write him and tell your grandfather really *is* very ill?"

"Don't you dare!" Alma protested. "You keep out of this. I don't need any meddling to help me cop my man! I'll get him, don't you worry."

"Oh, I'm not worrying," Dr. Jordan assured her hastily, "at least not about you. It's your fiancé who makes me feel that maybe he might need a bit of help to resist your wiles."

"He's doing all right without any help," said Alma grimly. "There's just one thing I want from you, Cole Jordan; and that's to get my Gramps up and on his feet and out of here as fast as possible."

"That we will, my dear, that we will," Dr. Jordan assured her. As she turned and went down the stairs, he followed her with his eyes, and when he turned back Leona was surprised at his expression, though he said casually enough, "That's quite a gal, that is."

"She surely is," Leona agreed. "And a beauty, too."

Dr. Jordan nodded agreement as he smiled at her and went on to complete his before-lunch rounds.

By the time set for Lamar's phlebotomy Leona felt that she had been at Cypress General for ages. She had settled into her work and was now able to take the place in the operating room for which she had been engaged.

Dr. Foster was still curt and brusque with her. But by now she had found that this was his usual attitude toward all those with whom she came in contact, and so she no longer minded. Her admiration and respect for his skill increased with each operation on which she served with him.

The little Jennings girl was recovering nicely, Jane had told her. The tumor had been benign, and she would be going home soon.

The phlebotomy on Lamar Pruitt was a delicate one, and Leona knew that he would be on the "critical list" for several days at least. As his special duty nurse, it was part of her job to keep Alma out of the room, since there must be no visitors for the first three or four days. And she found that almost as difficult as tending her patient.

"I won't bother him," Alma pleaded tearfully. "I won't scold him or yell at him; I won't even weep over him. I just want to *see* him."

At such times Dr. Jordan was usually around, and many times in those critical days, Leona had good reason to be grateful to Dr. Jordan and to what Jane had called "his way with the gals". Each time Alma burst into tears, Dr. Jordan would soothe her back to composure.

At last came the midnight hour when Lamar passed the crisis and could be removed from the "critical list". And Alma was allowed to pay him a five-minute visit; and then to make longer calls.

Leona came along the corridor one afternoon after she had been relieved of her special duty with Lamar and heard voices coming from his room. She opened the door and peeped in.

Lamar saw her and called out in a surprisingly strong voice, "So there you are! You've deserted me, abandoned me. Where have you been?"

Alma, in riding breeches and boots, sat sprawled in a chair, one leg draped over the arm. A tall, sandy-haired young man lounging against the window seat straightened and stood up.

"Are we making too much noise, Nurse?" he asked anxiously, his blue-gray eyes sweeping over the pretty picture she made in her immaculate white uniform.

"Oh, no," Leona answered him, smiling. "I just came in to check on Mr. Pruitt, though I'm sure Mrs. Hastings is taking wonderful care of him."

"Oh, Hasty's a good egg," Alma said. "But Gramps misses you. I told you he had an eye for a pretty girl."

Leona laughed. "I've been busy in surgery," she told Lamar.

Lamar nodded. "Oh, well, I suppose they do need their best nurse in the operating room."

Leona made a gay courtesy as she took the chart from the foot of the bed and glanced at it with swift approval.

"Why, thank you sir," she mocked lightly.

"I'm Bruce McClain," said the sandy-haired young man.

"Well, hold your hossess, pardner; I was about to introduce you." Alma chuckled. "Leona Gregory, Bruce McClain. And I hope you'll become the very best of friends."

"I hope so, too," Bruce said eagerly.

"Bruce McClain?" Leona repeated, because somewhere in her mind the name seemed to ring a bell.

"Uncle Dan's great-nephew and heir," Alma explained kindly.

"Oh, I've heard so much about your uncle since I came here," said Leona. "You must be very proud of him."

"Very sorry I never had the privilege of knowing him," Bruce said. "Maybe he could have told me what he wants me to do with the property he left. I feel like such a fool when I realize that the most ignorant Seminole on the place knows more than I do about what should be done about things."

"Oh, you're doing fine, my boy," said Lamar. "Uncle Dan would have been very happy to see you buckle down and carry on."

"Thanks," said Bruce, and his unhandsome, squarecut face was touched with a grateful smile. "I'd never have managed without your and Alma's help."

"Well, there's always Carol," Alma said gently, a hint of malice in her eyes. "Oh, boy, is there always Carol!"

"Now stop lambasting the girl," Lamar protested. "Carol's not that bad."

"And how bad is that?" asked Alma with frank interest.

"Not bad enough to justify all the spiteful things you and others say about her," said her grandfather firmly.

"She's trying her darnedest to marry Bruce," Alma pointed out reasonably, and Bruce stiffened.

"Now see here, Alma," he began.

Alma shrugged and tapped her polished boot with her riding crop.

"Well, of course it's none of my business. If you want the girl to marry you all you'll have to do is wave your little finger."

Leona said, "I really must go. Is there anything I can do for you, Mr. Pruitt? I have an hour off and I'd be glad to—"

Behind her there was a gentle tap at the closed door, and Leona swung it open to admit the prettiest girl she had ever seen; a girl with silver-gilt hair framing a small, heart-shaped face with a cleft in the chin and eyes so blue that they were like sapphires. The girl wore a thin white frock that molded an exquisite, doll-like figure and high-heeled strapped slippers, and the armful of peach-colored gladioli in her arms made her look like a girl on a calendar.

"Oh," she stammered like an abashed child as she saw Bruce and Alma, "I'm afraid I'm intruding. I just wanted to bring Uncle Lamar these flowers to cheer him up."

She held out the flowers to Leona, who accepted them with a smile and murmured something about getting a vase for them. As she turned to leave the room, Alma said, without the slightest trace of warmth in her voice, "Leona, this is Carol Decker, who lives at the McClain place. Leona is the surgical nurse here, Carol, and was Gramps' special while he was so ill."

"How do you do, Nurse?" said Carol in a soft, child-like voice. "Alma forgot to tell you that Mother is the McClain housekeeper and I'm practically a maid."

"Oh, for Pete's sake, Carol," protested Alma uncomfortably.

"But I've known Uncle Lamar since I was a baby," Carol went on sweetly, "and I've been terribly worried about him. So this afternoon when I had to come in to do the marketing, I went out and cut these flowers for him. They're lovely, aren't they? Uncle Dan planted them, and he always loved them."

"They are lovely, Carol and it was sweet of you to bring them," said Lamar.

"It was my pleasure, Uncle Lamar," said Carol earnestly. "And I do hope you'll be back home soon; we miss you. I'd better go now and do the marketing. It's been nice seeing you, Uncle Lamar, and you, too, Alma."

Alma nodded without answering. Leona saw a faint touch of color rise in the girl's lovely face; as she turned away, her eyes caught and held Bruce's somewhat uneasy gaze.

"Will you be home for dinner, Brucie?" she asked wistfully.

"He will not," Alma stated flatly before Bruce could answer. "He's taking me to dinner, and we may very easily be quite late, so don't wait up for him."

Carol's jaw set, and for just a moment

the wistful sweetness melted from her eyes and there was a tiny flash.

"Oh, then mother and I will eat in the kitchen where we belong, and we wouldn't dare wait up for Brucie!"

She went out, leaving behind her an uneasy silence.

"Did you have to be so rough on her, baby?" asked Lamar.

"Now don't you go feeling sorry for her!" snapped Alma. "She's so sorry for herself that for anybody else to feel sorry for her would be just a bit too much!"

"I feel like a heel," Bruce admitted ruefully. "She and her mother lived out there with Uncle Dan and took care of him for twenty years; and yet the property was left to me, and I never even knew the old gentleman."

"They were well paid for everything they ever did for Uncle Dan," Alma protested. "He educated Carol, and she had the prettiest clothes of any girl in high school. She could have gone away to college if she had wanted to, but Carol is too lazy-minded to want that. She just wanted Cypress Groves, and when she found he'd left the place to you, she decided if she couldn't inherit the property she would marry it! And if you don't watch your step that's exactly what she's going to do! Is that what you want?"

"Good Lord, no!" Bruce gasped in panic.

"Well, you'd sure better walk warily, m'boy. That's exactly what she has in mind. I've tried to warn you. I've even been willing to cooperate with you by letting her think you're madly in love with me, even though I *do* have a man who's going to be mine just as soon as I can beat some sense into his head," Alma told him.

Lamar said warily, "Maybe he's already got sense enough not to want to be captured by a drivin' female like you."

Alma's careless gesture tossed that thought into the nearest wastebasket.

"Oh, he's madly in love with me and would marry me like a shot if it weren't that he has some cockeyed idea that he has no right to marry me until he is able to support me in the style to which you've accustomed me," she answered, and looked at her grandfather. "I suppose you wouldn't care to disinherit me so I can go and starve with him and live happy ever after?"

"I would not," her grandfather told her firmly. "You'll inherit Palmadora, and you'll run the estate just as you've been trained to do since you were knee-high to a grasshopper. Think I'm going to let the place go to seed, allow all the people who depend on their jobs to suffer, just so you can run off and marry some man who's too stiff-necked with pride to want you if you own Palmadora? Not a chance, my girl, not a chance."

Alma nodded as though she hadn't expected anything else. She heaved a deep sigh as she rose to her feet with a single fluid lovely movement and absently brushed off the rest of her riding breeches.

"So there you are, Brucie my dear." She managed a coo that was a devastating parody of Carol's low, self-consciously sweet voice. "Either you pay frantic attention to me and pretend to be besotted about me; or you'll be gobbled up by the limp and lovely Carol. The choice, my friend, is yours."

"Oh, I've made my choice," Bruce assured her hastily. "I'm very grateful for your protection. Alma, if you're quite sure your fiancé won't object?"

Alma sniffed.

"My fiancé my foot!" she scoffed bitterly. "He couldn't care less! Oh, he's in love with me. But he won't be a rich woman's husband, and Gramps won't disinherit me. So I may as well do what I can to protect you from the frail and lovely Carol. Frail? She's about as frail as a hundred-year-old tortoise."

Lamar had been watching Leona's face as she stood holding the gladioli, and suddenly he chuckled.

"I'd give a pretty penny, Leona, to know what you're thinking about all this," he told her.

Leona laughed. "Oh, I have the feeling that it's the middle of a movie and I haven't the faintest idea what happened before or what's going to happen next. So I'm just a completely detached observer."

Alma eyed her swiftly.

"I know what you're thinking," she accused the girl. "You think I'm a mean, malicious, spiteful cat and that poor little Carol doesn't deserve all the ugly things I've been saying about her. But believe me, Leona, I've known Carol since kindergarten days when we used to throw rocks at each other and spill each other's finger paint. Carol's a real weirdie. People would like her if she'd only let them; she's a real beauty and could be a lot of fun. But she has this inferiority complex. Just because her mother was Uncle Dan's housekeeper, she's so sure she's going to be snubbed if she dares lift her head that she snubs first."

"She's really a lovely girl," said Leona.

"She looks like a girl in search of a dream," Alma agreed. "And so she is— the dream of being rich and snooty and stepping on everybody who gets in her way. As mistress of Cypress Groves she could have realized that dream. And it's a dream she hasn't given up now that she knows Bruce is unmarried."

She thrust her hands into the pockets of her riding breeches and stood balanced, feet apart, looking at Bruce.

"Poor Bruce!" she mocked him. "Under the same roof with a girl whose intentions are strictly honorable, because she hates you only a little less than she hates everybody else in the world."

"What did she do to you, girl, that you hate her so?" asked Lamar quietly.

Alma turned swiftly to face him, startled.

"Why, Gramps, I don't hate her," she protested.

"Well, it's pretty obvious that you aren't exactly crazy about her,"Lamar pointed out.

Alma shook her head, and the short, crisp black curls that were confined by a bright red ribbon danced in the light.

"No," she admitted, "I don't like her. She won't let people like her. She's darned near a mental case in her attitude toward everybody else in the world. Let's not talk about her any more. All I'm trying to do is to keep her from sneaking up on Bruce's blind side and marrying him before he knows what's happening."

Nettled, as any man would have been under the circumstances, Bruce said swiftly, "Well, now look, don't you suppose a man can protect himself in such a situation? No girl can marry a man against his will."

Alma stared at him as though he had made an incredibly stupid remark. Then she turned and looked at Leona, and there was a twinkle of amusement in her eyes.

"How naïve can a man get? You heard what he said, didn't you?"

Bruce looked swiftly at Leona and colored faintly as she met his look with a smile.

"I heard him, Alma," said Leona. "And I think he's right."

Lamar chuckled aloud and Bruce looked pleased, but Alma was outraged.

"What?" she gasped. "For Pete's sake,

Leona, where've you been since you grew up? Don't you know no man alive has the slightest thing to say in his defense when a girl really makes up her mind to marry him?"

She heard her grandfather's chuckle and turned swiftly, head erect, eyes blazing.

"So all right, I haven't landed my man yet, but I will! Make no mistake about that," she said hotly. "I'll wear him down, you wait and see. But until then I'm glad to help Bruce escape from the wiles of the Clinging Vine. Shall we get started, Brucie m' boy?"

"Yes, ma'am," Bruce answered firmly, "but only on one condition."

Alma elevated her eyebrows questioningly.

"And that is?" she asked.

"That you stop calling me Brucie!"

"But Carol dear calls you Brucie," Alma reminded him.

"From her I have to take it because I haven't been able to talk her out of it," Bruce answered. "But you I like, and from you I won't take it. And that's final."

There was raillery in Alma's eyes, though she answered demurely. "Spoken like a little gentleman. You've talked me into it. Bruce it is."

She tucked her hand though Bruce's arm. The two of them faced Lamar, and Leona told herself they made a very handsome couple.

"Well, enjoy your rest cure, Lazy Bones," Alma told Lamar briskly. "And when you do stir your lazy self out of that bed and come on home, don't blame me if things are in a mess at the ranch. After all, I'm only a lone, lorn female with two left hands and part of a brain."

"You're frightening me, chick." Lamar laughed. "That part of a brain of yours works like a steel trap, and we both know you could run Palmadora better than any two men alive."

Alma nodded thoughtfully and glanced at Bruce.

"Um, maybe so," she agreed. "But you're a stinker to say so in front of

Bruce, who admires the helpless, clinging vine type."

Bruce asked Lamar with interest, "Did you ever wallop her when she was a kid, Mr. Pruitt?"

Lamar's saggy white brows went up in shock.

"I wouldn't have dared!" he confessed.

"I thought not," Bruce said. "You've sure made it tough for her husband. He'll have to smack her down twice a day and three times on Sunday to knock some of the brashness out of her."

"Phooey!" sniffed Alma. "Such a man should be born."

They went away, and Leona heard their laughter as they descended the stairs.

6

AS the days slid swiftly past, Leona found herself more and more a part of the busy routine of the hospital. She came to know the other RNs and the PNs as well; the interns, the attendants, the entire staff. She made friends among them as she had in the case of Jane Lester in the charity ward. She found deep satisfaction in the knowledge that she was doing a good job, and now and then Dr. Foster gave her a word of praise. And because such words were scarce she appreciated them all the more. Paula was not quite so brusque, but still the rigid disciplinarian her job required.

Dr. Jordan had dated her occasionally, as often as their busy schedule permitted, and had talked of his plans once his internship at the hospital should be finished.

On the day that Lamar was discharged

100

from the hospital, Alma announced blithely that she was giving a small party for him to welcome him home the following Sunday afternoon at Palmadora.

"You and Cole are invited," she told Leona joyously. "And there'll be Bruce and me. We'll just have a simple, informal party. I'd ask you out for lunch, but I know your duty hours on Sunday and that you won't be free, either of you, until after three. So I thought we'd make it a buffet supper beside the pool and not get Gramps too excited, as he would be if I tried to make it a formal dinner party. I'm putting him to bed at eight o'clock, and he'd fight me if I made him leave the dinner table that early."

"I'd love to come, if I can get Dr. Foster's permission to be away for a couple of hours," Leona admitted.

"Oh, that's all been arranged," Alma told her casually. "You and Cole can be away from the hospital from three p.m. until eight-thirty. I promised Dr. F. that if there should be an emergency and you were needed earlier, I'd rush you back fast."

Leona's eyes widened. "Well, in that case, thanks a lot. I can't speak for Dr. Jordan, of course."

Alma tilted her pretty head and grinned impishly.

"I can! He'll be delighted," she drawled. "He wants the good will of the Pruitts when he sets up shop for himself here in the fall."

"Now look," Leona protested warmly, "I refuse to believe that Dr. Jordan can be bribed."

"Oh, my eye!" Alma mocked her, and laughed as she went hurrying out to the car where her grandfather waited.

And so on Sunday afternoon when she had completed her duties and was free for her rest period, Leona dressed in a thin cool cotton frock the color of young poplar leaves in spring. It was, she told herself happily as she smoothed the filmy soft frock over her slender hips, nice to be out of uniform for a while.

Dr. Jordan was waiting for her when

she came down the stairs, and his eyes lit up as he looked at her.

"Well, well, well, the Spring Maid herself," he greeted her. "Am I ever going to be proud to wear you on my arm!"

"The feeling, sir, is mutual." Leona laughed as her eyes swept over him: tall, tanned and terrific in pale beige slacks and a jacket of a shade darker of shantung.

They emerged from the hospital into a blaze of brilliant sunshine, and as they walked toward his car, Leona lifted her face to the sun's caress and said happily, "I just don't believe it's late March! It's more like June or July."

"And you've been here almost two months and haven't worked a bit on your sun-tan! Scandalous, my girl, scandalous!" he mocked her.

"Well, you're tanned enough for both of us." Leona studied him with mocking curiosity. "What *is* that shade you're wearing? Seminole copper, or Cordovan brown?"

Dr. Jordan put her into his car and slid beneath the wheel.

"Oh, it's a shade that's meant to impress the tourists, of whom we don't get half enough," he told her. "The local people think I'm too pale; the visitors wonder how long it takes to get this brown."

"It's very becoming," Leona told him demurely.

"Well, aren't you a sweet child to say so!" Dr. Jordan grinned.

Leona settled herself in the seat beside him and watched the scenery as it slid by.

"Wait until June when the poincianas bloom," Cole told her. "They're really something to see. The jacarandas, too, and the allamandas. Those are something we natives keep for ourselves; the winter visitors are gone long before that so we can revel in their beauty all by ourselves."

"I can hardly wait." Leona sighed happily.

"You'll be here in June and July, of course?"

She looked up at him, puzzled by his question.

"I'll be here until next February," she told him. "I signed a year's contract."

"Good! By that time I should have my office all set up, and maybe I can persuade you to come and work with me," said Dr. Jordan.

"I don't think so, Cole," she said quietly.

She met his swift glance and added, "I don't want to be a 'luxury nurse', tending the imaginary ailments of people whose chief trouble is too much money and too much spare time."

Dr. Jordan's hands tightened on the wheel and his jaw stiffened.

"So you don't feel that the rich and well-heeled are entitled to a doctor's best efforts?" he asked dryly.

"Well, of course I do," Leona protested. "But people who are poor and unable to pay exorbitant fees are also entitled to a doctor's best efforts, aren't they? And a nurse's?"

"I see you've been listening to gossip

about me, Leona," he said. "It's quite true that I intend to be what you call a 'luxury doctor' and give my very best services to people who are able to pay what you call 'exhorbitant fees'. Leona, I have to make money, a whole lot of money, and fast!"

She was startled at his tone, the bleakness in his eyes.

"Medicine happens to be the one thing I'm good at, and I've worked very hard to learn my trade. Is it so disgusting that now I have learned it, to the best of my ability, I want to make a lot of money from it?"

"Of course not," she flashed warmly. "I didn't say it was disgusting."

"Your implication was plain," said Dr. Jordan grimly, and added before she could answer, "Here we are."

The car turned from the paved road between two large coquina-rock pillars bearing the name, "Palmadora Ranch". They rode along a wide, curving drive that ran between tall Australian pines, beside a circular sweep of lawn where palm trees stood with their fronds stirring softly in a scarcely perceptible breeze.

The house itself was built in the Spanish style.

As they came to a halt beside the hacienda, Alma came running to meet them, wearing a brief white bathing suit beneath a giant beach towel slung carelessly about her brown shoulders.

"Well, here you are at last," she greeted them exuberantly, as Bruce, also in swimming attire and a beach shirt, followed her. "I was afraid you'd be too late for a swim. But the water's warm enough. What detained you? I thought surely there must have been an emergency at the hospital."

She gave them no time to answer as she slid a hand through Leona's arm, laughed up at Dr. Jordan and drew them with her to the pool glinting through the dappled sunlit shade.

Bruce grinned at Leona.

"Hello again," he said happily.

"Hello." Leona let him take her arm

from Alma's grasp and enclosed it in his own.

Alma glanced at him, then at Dr. Jordan, and laughed.

"Come along, Cole m'boy," she drawled. "These two want to be alone, seems as if."

"I'm not sure I approve of that," objected Dr. Jordan.

"Now that should cause them a vast deal of worry, I'm sure," Alma teased him.

Lamar was sitting in a deep beach chair, his legs elevated on the foot rest. He, too, wore bathing attire, but it was quite dry, and Alma answered Dr. Jordan's protest before he could make it.

"Oh, he hasn't been in the pool. I wouldn't allow it. He begged and begged, but I said, 'No, siree, no pool for you!'" She looked up at Dr. Jordan with pretended anxiety, "Did I do right, Doc?"

"Quite right, miss. I couldn't have done better myself," Dr. Jordan told her.

"There now, Gramps!" said Alma.

"You see? I told you the doc wouldn't want you in the pool."

"Been a long time since I took orders from a snip, like you," Lamar growled at her.

"Come on, Leona. You've got time for a swim before supper, and I'm sure there's a bathing suit that will fit you." Alma urged her guest toward the small cabaña at the back of the pool, that was partially screened by giant double hibiscus glowing ruby-red in the sunlight. "Cole, you know where to find your own."

It was a lovely afternoon, and Leona reveled in it. The water of the pool, milk-warm, felt satin-soft against her body; it was quite deep at one end, and she was able to swim the length and back several times.

They had all pulled themselves out of the pool and were perched on the edge, busy with beach towels, when a car came swiftly up the drive.

Alma stared and stiffened.

"Oh, no, it can't be," she muttered.

"She wouldn't dare try to crash the party when I didn't invite her."

"Oh, my stars and bars," Leona heard Bruce mutter even before the car came to a halt and the door opened.

Carol, in powder-blue linen, her silver-gilt hair ruffled by the faint wind, came hurrying to them, her spike heels threatening to trip her in the shell-strewn drive.

"Oh, hello, Carol," Alma purred. "Come to borrow a cup of sugar, I imagine?"

Leona saw ugly color creep into the girl's exquisite face before she got herself under control and shook her head.

"I didn't come to crash your party, Alma," she said huskily. "I came for Bruce. Starlight's acting up again, and Sam can't handle him, and he asked me to get Brucie as fast as I could."

"And the telephone was out of order?" asked Alma with polite interest.

But Bruce was on his feet.

"I'll change, Carol, and be right home. Thanks for coming for me," he told her, and ran off to the cabaña.

Alma and Carol exchanged long, level looks while the others sat in awkward discomfort.

"I'm truly sorry, Alma, that I spoiled your party," Carol offered a painfully humble apology. "But you know how crazy Brucie is about Starlight. I don't know what he would do if anything serious happened to him."

"And what's about to happen to Starlight now?" asked Alma politely.

"Well, he's kicked the stall out and is running loose in the field and Sam can't get him back to the stable," Carol offered eagerly. "And although Starlight is kicking so Sam can't be sure, he thinks the horse cut his leg when he kicked the stall down."

"Starlight seems to be on quite a rampage," drawled Alma. As Bruce came hurrying from the cabaña, she stood up. "Come on, Leona, Cole; let's go along and see the fun."

Swift alarm dawned in Carol's eyes and she said hastily, "Oh, that won't be

111

necessary. I'm quite sure Brucie can handle him."

"I am, too," said Alma cheerfully. "But it ought to be something to see. Gramps, we'll be back in time for supper. You behave yourself now."

"That's advice you might do well to take yourself," Lamar answered.

Alma flashed him a glance and wrinkled her nose impudently at him. As Bruce came up, she slid her hand through his arm and said gaily, "We're all going along, Brucie dear. And as soon as you get Starlight settled down we'll come back to supper."

"Oh, good," said Bruce happily, and smiled at Leona. "I'd like you to see Starlight, Leona. He's really a beauty."

"But it's really not necessary," Carol was still protesting even as Alma, Leona and Dr. Jordan approached the waiting station wagon.

Leona noted that as they reached the station wagon, Carol manoeuvered herself so that when she, Alma and Bruce got into the front seat, Carol was in the middle. As Dr. Jordan helped Leona into his own car, he winked at her and called to the others, "Leona and I will follow; then we can bring you two back after the shenanigans are over."

Alma called something, but they could not hear her as the station wagon went pelting off down the drive.

After a while they came to a split-rail fence, with two huge wagon wheels in lieu of gates.

Dr. Jordan drove through the gates, and they came in sight of the house. Leona's eyes widened. The hacienda at Palmadora had been a gracious, dignified, even stately looking place. But this house was a pioneer house; built at least a hundred years ago, perhaps more. It was big and gaunt-looking, and the timbers had been silvered by weather. There was a wide veranda on three sides, and one corner was half-smothered with blossoming vines that sent out a faint but exquisite fragrance that was almost smothered by the cloying smell of citrus blossoms.

"Uncle Dan's family built it when they first came down here," Dr. Jordan answered her suprised look. "He was just a little boy; he grew up here. It was home and he loved it. He used to boast that there wasn't a nail in it. All heart pine, he said, and put together with hand-carved pegs. He also used to boast that it wasn't built by slave labor. Uncle Dan hated slavery, and so did his father and his grandfather. They brought down a couple of master carpenters, and the rest of the work was done by the Seminoles."

He had slowed the car, his eyes on the station wagon ahead. Then the station-wagon moved on and Dr. Jordan followed, down a winding private road to a neat row of stable buildings. There was an exercise yard, and beyond that another space where horses and cattle grazed peacefully.

As Bruce stopped the station wagon and jumped out, a tall, copper-skinned man in clean but faded khaki breeches and shirt came to meet him. He took off his wide-brimmed hat and thrust his fingers through crewcut coarse black hair.

"Sorry you had to be rushed over here, Mr. Bruce." He spoke in a warm, mellow voice. "I tried to persuade Miss Carol not to go after you. But she was afraid something might happen to Starlight, and she knew how much you think of him."

"What happened, Sam?" asked Bruce.

"Why, nothing much, Mr. Bruce," said Sam awkwardly, carefully avoiding Carol's blazing eyes. "He just kicked a bit and got out of the stable and went racing off down the pasture. He hasn't been ridden in a couple of days, and I suppose he's a bit restless."

"He wasn't hurt?" asked Bruce.

"Why, no, Mr. Bruce." Sam seemed puzzled by the question.

Bruce turned swiftly to Carol, who took a backward step from the anger in his eyes.

"You said he had injured his leg," he accused her.

Feeling Alma's amused, somewhat

contemptuous eyes on her, Carol said sharply, "Sam said he had."

"Oh, no, Miss Carol. You must have misunderstood me," Sam protested.

Carol flared on him as though grateful to have an object for the fury she could no longer control.

"Are you calling me a liar, Sam?" she blazed.

"Oh, now wait a minute, Carol," Bruce put in wearily.

"I'm only saying you misunderstood me, Miss Carol, that's all." Sam spoke as though he had not heard Bruce's attempt to ease the tension. "Going after Mr. Bruce was your idea, not mine, remember?"

Carol swung a swift, beseeching glance about the group that was warching her curiously, and then her eyes came back to Bruce's and clung, and there was a mist of tears in them.

"I'm sorry," she stammered faintly. "I know how much Starlight means to you. Nobody else here can handle him, so I thought maybe you'd better come and get him back in the stable."

"You think it's necessary to stable him again before night, Sam?" Bruce asked.

"No, Mr. Bruce. He's having a wonderful time. But you're going to have to ride him good and hard tomorrow. He's spoiling for exercise," Sam answered.

"I'll do that, Sam," said Bruce, obviously relieved, and turned to Alma. "Sorry we spoiled your party, Alma honey, but it seemed like an emergency."

"The party's not spoiled, don't be silly," Alma told him gaily and tucked her hand through his arm. "Shall we get started back? Gramps will be worried about Starlight, since he's to blame for you buying him."

She glanced at Carol. "Won't you join us, Carol? We'd love to have you."

"I just bet you would!" Carol's carefully maintained pose of sweet submissiveness had disappeared completely, and she faced them like an angry, spitting cat, her hands clenched, her face white and twisted with anger. "Oh, sure, you'll be kind to the poor little kitchen maid while you're laughing like fools because I take my duties here seriously. This is Bruce's place, and Mother and I have always been taught just where our responsibilities lie. No, thanks, *Duchess!* The kitchen maid has no desire to mingle with her betters!"

Alma was staring at her, wide-eyed. Without giving anybody a chance to answer her, Carol turned and went running blindly toward the house.

"Well, do tell!" Alma murmured when the shadows of the deep back porch had swallowed Carol up. "I honestly didn't mean to hurt her feelings."

"Didn't you?" asked Dr. Jordan dryly, and turned away from her hurt, startled look. "Let's have a look at this famous hawss, McClain. Where is he?"

Bruce walked back to the fence and gave a low whistle. Down at the lower end of the field, where several horses grazed, one lifted his head and whickered. Bruce whistled again, and the horse came forward. He was a magnificent beast, his black coat shining in the sunlight and the great white blaze on his forehead setting him apart from the other horses.

Bruce whistled again, but the horse came no closer. He merely stood watching Bruce, and then he turned and went back to the others and began cropping the tender green grass.

"Arrogant beast, isn't he?" drawled Dr. Jordan.

"Oh, well, he's afraid I'll stable him again," Bruce explained the horse's refusal to come closer.

"Well-trained, just like Carol," mused Alma teasingly. "One word from you and he does exactly as he pleases."

"He hasn't had enough exercise lately," Sam apologized for the beast.

"I'll give him a good hard run tomorrow and teach him who's boss," Bruce boasted. "Isn't he a beauty?"

"He's magnificent," Leona said eagerly. "I'd have been terrified if he had come any closer, though."

"That's your cue, Brucie darling, to

say, 'Why, he's gentle as a kitten!'" Alma mocked.

"That he isn't, Miss Pruitt. He can be really hard to handle. I'm a little uneasy about him myself," Sam said firmly, and grinned at them, his teeth very white in his copper-colored face. "Sorry you had to rush back, Mr. Bruce."

"I'm not." Bruce chuckled. "I always welcome a chance to show off Starlight. And I wasn't quite sure whether I dared invite you folks out for a party, since Carol was being—well, shall we say a bit difficult?"

"Oh, let's say that by all means," Alma said cheerfully. "Only it's the understatement of the century! Come on; let's get traveling."

With her hand on Bruce's arm, she walked with him to the station wagon. Dr. Jordan watched them with a cynical smile before he turned to Leona.

"There's something frightening in two women fighting over a man. At the moment my sympathies are with Carol. She hasn't got a dog's chance, with Alma around. Alma's a very knowledgeable gal, you see," he drawled.

"You believe she's really interested in Bruce, don't you?" Leona asked slowly as they moved back to his car and the station wagon went off down the drive.

"What a question! Don't you?" asked Dr. Jordan as he slid beneath the wheel and started the car.

"But what about the man in Tampa?" asked Leona uneasily.

Dr. Jordan slanted an amused glance at her.

"Is there a man in Tampa? I mean one Alma wants?" he drawled.

7

IT was perhaps a week later that a call came for an ambulance to be sent to Cypress Groves immediately. Bruce had been thrown and trampled by Starlight and his injuries were serious, if not critical.

Dr. Jordan went with the ambulance while Leona and Dr. Foster and the operating room technicians prepared for the arrival of the patient. When he was brought in, Leona was beside him, and though he seemed in a daze he managed to whisper to her, "Not Starlight's fault. . . . Mine. Don't let anything happen to Starlight."

"Of course we won't," Leona soothed him as he was lifted to the operating table and the anesthetist began administering the anesthesia.

Once more Leona admired and respected the speed and skill with which

Dr. Foster worked, with Dr. Jordan assisting. The circulating nurses stood back, well out of the way yet instantly alert should there by any need of their services. Leona stood beside Dr. Foster, watchful, ready to hand him without his asking whatever instruments he needed.

There were massive head injuries, a smashed collarbone and, much more serious, the danger of damage to spine. Leona held her breath when Dr. Foster began probing delicately for the bone splinter that he was sure must be there, ready to do its deadly, crippling work if it was not found and removed. And when she saw the tiny splinter in the forceps and saw the glint of pleasure in Dr. Foster's eyes, she felt like cheering. Instead she only met Dr. Foster's eyes and knew that the delight in her own told him how she rejoiced at his skill and competence.

It was a long and tedious operation. When at last it was over, and the patient was being wheeled very gently to the recovery room, a circulating nurse carrying the blood-plasma bottle ever so gently so that there would be no interruption of the delivery of the life-giving fluid, Leona stripped off her mask and looked up at Dr. Foster with shining eyes.

"You're wonderful!" she breathed, and for almost the first time saw a slight smile on Dr. Foster's usually stern face and knew he was pleased.

"Well, thanks, I had expert assistance," he answered, and nodded at Dr. Jordan. "Good work, Cole. And you, too, Nurse."

"If he lives and rides again, Dr. F., he'll have you to thank for it," said Dr. Jordan firmly.

"It's part of our job, Cole," said Dr. Foster, and seemed to feel there was no more to be said. "He'll need special nursing, Miss Gregory. He'll be in your charge."

"Thank you, Doctor. I'll do my best," Leona said eagerly.

"I'm sure you will. He's a friend of yours, isn't he?" asked Dr. Foster so unexpectedly that despite her weariness

Leona felt the color rise in her face and knew Dr. Jordan was looking at her sharply.

"Well, yes, I've met him a few times," she answered hurriedly, "at the Pruitts' and here when Mr. Pruitt was ill."

"He's Uncle Dan's nephew *and* heir," observed Dr. Jordan dryly, his eyes still on Leona's telltale flush.

"Well, if he were an ignorant backwoods fisherman, we'd still do our best for him," said Dr. Foster curtly. "There's no partiality here at Harbor Hospital."

He walked out. Dr. Jordan eyed Leona for a moment, then shrugged as he turned away to clean up after the job. Leona watched him as one of the circulating nurses untied the ties of his surgeon's gown and accepted the cap and mask he took off before he disappeared into the scrub room.

Suddenly there was a wild keening outside, and Leona and the circulating nurse looked at each other, startled. The door popped open and a ward nurse thrust her head inside and said anxiously,

"Somebody come and convince Miss Decker that he's going to live."

"Good heavens, is that Carol Decker making all that fuss?" protested the circulating nurse in a tone of disgust. "Does she think he's the only patient in the hospital, for Pete's sake?"

"I'll talk to her," Leona offered, and hurried out.

Carol was in the lobby, having been prevented from climbing the stairs. She was wailing and screaming, and Alma, torn between disgust and anxiety, was trying to quiet her.

Leona, still wearing her gown and operating room cap came swiftly down the stairs, laid her hands on Carol's arms and felt the girl quiver beneath her touch.

"Stop it this minute, Carol, do you hear me?" Leona ordered sternly. "There's one sure way to cure hysteria, you know."

"I wanted to swat her," Alma said frankly. "But I didn't trust myself not to hit too hard. There's a penalty for murder in this state."

"He's going to be all right, Carol. Do

you understand? He's going to be all right! Dr. Foster did a marvelous job, and he's in the recovery room right this minute," Leona told the sobbing girl.

"You're not lying to me?" Carol whimpered.

"Of course not, Carol."

"He wasn't dead when they got here with him?"

"Of course he wasn't. He's badly banged up, of course, and he may be here for several weeks. But by that time he'll be as good as new," Leona assured her so firmly that Carol finally stopped sobbing.

A PN came hurrying with a glass of milky-looking liquid which Carol swallowed like an obedient child, while the others watched her uneasily.

"It was that horrible horse, Starlight," Carol hiccoughed at last. "I'm going straight back to the ranch and order him destroyed!"

"Oh, no, Carol, you mustn't!" Leona protested while Alma merely looked shocked.

Some of Carol's old animosity came

back. "Oh, *musn't* I! And who's going to stop me, I'd like to know? When Brucie isn't at the ranch, Mother and I give the orders. And Starlight's going to be shot just as soon as I can get back out there!"

She jerked herself free of Leona's attempted restraint and went running out of the hospital. A moment later they heard the spatter of shells from the drive that indicated the speed of her departure.

Leona cried out in sharp dismay, "Oh, Alma, she mustn't!"

"Afraid you made a mistake telling her so, honey," Alma said ruefully. "The slightest hint of opposition is all that it takes to send Carol careening off into some wild activity."

"But, Alma, Bruce was conscious for a moment or so while we were preparing him for surgery," Leona explained swiftly. "So I know he doesn't want the horse destroyed. He said it was his fault and begged me not to let anything happen to Starlight."

"Are you sure?" asked Alma urgently.

"Well, of course I'm sure," Leona

protested. "How could I not be sure when it's a part of a nurse's job to catch the faintest whisper from a patient and try to do what he asks?"

"Then we've got to get out to the ranch," said Alma swiftly.

"I can't leave."

"You'll have to," Alma said. "It will be your word against hers. If I tell Sam what *you* told me Bruce said, and then she gives the order—well, you can understand. Sam will take your word, but you'll have to give it to him personally. Scoot now and change."

"But, Alma, Dr. Foster—" Leona protested anxiously.

"You change! I'll talk to Dr. F. Now get along," ordered Alma.

Leona fled up the stairs. When she returned a few minutes later in her uniform, Dr. Foster was scowling at Alma, who was talking urgently to him.

Dr. Foster turned to Leona and said curtly, "You may go, since Alma feels it's of such importance to the eventual good of the patient. Dr. Jordan can keep an eye on him, and there are the recovery room nurses. But get back here as fast as you can."

"Oh, I'll get back as fast as the law allows," Alma promised; "maybe even faster."

"The legal speed limit, Alma, please. Miss Gregory is much too important a personage here at the hospital to run the risk of her being smashed up in a car wreck," said Dr. Foster. As Leona ran out with Alma to where Alma's station wagon was parked, Leona felt a warm glow at Dr. Foster's words.

The two girls practically tumbled into the car, which went racing down the drive and into the road leading to the ranch.

"Carol wouldn't really have that magnificent beast destroyed, would she, Alma?" Leona asked uneasily.

"Oh, wouldn't she? And she'd grin like the Cheshire cat while Starlight was breathing his last! I keep telling you, Leona: you don't really know this gal. Remember, I grew up with her," Alma answered. She sneaked the station wagon expertly around a huge truck and grinned impishly as the driver leaned out and swore at her.

"But Bruce was so distressed," Leona worried. "If he recovers consciousness and finds Starlight has been destroyed—!"

"And don't think she wouldn't enjoy that, too!" Alma said grimly. "Did you ever see a more disgusting exhibition than she put on there at the hospital? I have never in my life wanted so much to literally smack her witless! She couldn't have made more fuss if she'd been his wife, which, let's pray, is something that will never happen."

Ahead of them were the giant wagon wheels that served for a gate at Cypress Groves. Alma whirled the car through it and brought it to a screeching halt near the stables.

The scene before them held them both rigid with shock for a moment.

Carol stood at the fence, and just inside it, Sam stood with a shotgun raised. Beyond, two stable hands were holding the bridle of the black horse which was rearing and curveting, whinnying with terror and anger.

"No, no, Sam, wait!" Alma cried out as Sam raised the gun to his shoulder and took aim at the horse. "You mustn't, Sam, you mustn't!"

Sam dropped the gun and whirled swiftly about, and Leona saw that his copper-colored skin was gray and his face rigid and sick.

"Miss Pruitt!" The relief that swept his face brought back some of the color to it and made it look less like a graven copper coin. "Mr. Bruce is not dead?"

"Of course not, Sam, and you mustn't do anything to Starlight!" Alma panted.

Carol screamed in fury and took a step toward Alma, her hands drawn into claws as though she meant to leap on Alma like a scratching, clawing cat.

"You get out of here, Alma Pruitt!" she screamed. "What business have you got giving orders here? Go ahead and shoot the brute, Sam!"

Sam waited anxiously for whatever Alma might say.

"Sam, this is Miss Gregory, a nurse at the hospital, a surgical nurse who assisted at the operation of Mr. Bruce," Alma explained swiftly. "He asked her to be sure nothing happened to Starlight and said the accident was all his fault."

Sam looked anxiously at Leona.

"Is that right, Miss Gregory? Mr. Bruce said it was his fault?"

"Yes, Sam, and he was terribly distressed for fear something might happen to Starlight," Leona answered, and repeated as explicitly as she could word for word what Bruce had said.

Sam murmured some Seminole expression, grinned wryly at Alma and nodded.

"Well, I'm glad he realized the fault was his, Miss Pruitt, Miss Gregory," he said when he had drawn a deep breath. "We are all very fond of Mr. Bruce. We think he's just about the greatest. But— well, let's face it, Miss Pruitt. He's not exactly what you'd call an expert rider."

Alma's grin good-naturedly answered his.

"Not by several million light years, Sam," she agreed.

"But he's trying, Miss Pruitt. He's trying," Sam assured her eagerly. "I wish he wouldn't try quite so hard. He's determined to ride Starlight. We've tried to persuade him to take one of the older, gentler horses, but he's so crazy about Starlight he won't listen. And today he insisted on saddling the horse himself."

"And didn't get the girth tight enough, and when he mounted the saddle slipped, and that startled Starlight and he reared," Alma finished the explanation to Sam's obvious relief.

"Well, yes, Miss Pruitt, that's about the size of it," he agreed.

"That's all a pack of lies," Carol screamed furiously. "Starlight's mean and vicious and dangerous. And I order you, Sam, to shoot him!"

Sam's face was now completely devoid of any expression as he turned to her and said quietly, "Now, Miss Carol, the horse belongs to Mr. Bruce, and if he doesn't want him shot I really can't do it."

Carol lunged for the gun, crying furiously, "Well, I can!"

Sam avoided her so neatly, so gracefully that Leona was reminded of a figure in a dance.

"No, Miss Carol," he said quietly. And to the two stable hands who were trying to quiet the horse, "Turn him into the pasture, boys. He's been reprieved!"

The stable hands released their grip on the horse's bridle. One of them managed to get the bridle off the horse while the other neatly side-stepped flashing heels as the horse bolted toward the pasture where a group of other horses were grazing.

Carol whirled on Leona in a fury, and Leona felt a little sick at the way the girl's lovely face was contorted into a mask of bitter hatred.

"I won't forget this, Alma Pruitt!" she said through her teeth, her voice shaking. "Nor you, either, Leona Gregory. I'll get even with you two if it's the last thing I ever do! Humiliating me like this in front of the servants! Denying my authority; making me look a fool!"

She whirled on Leona before Alma could do more than give her a look of complete disgust.

"And as for you, Nurse Gregory," Carol's tone was insolent, "I'll get even with you, too. I'll make you wish you'd never been born! I'll make the hospital too hot to hold you! And don't think I can't!" she spat out, and went running to the house.

Leona and Alma watched her go, and then Alma made a wry grimace.

"Sorry I got you into this, Leona," she said apologetically.

"Well, for goodness sake Alma, I only gave the message Bruce wanted brought out here," Leona answered. "I'm afraid I can't be terribly upset by Carol's threats. If I am the kind of nurse she can get fired, then I don't deserve the job to begin with."

Alma turned to Sam. "You take good care of Starlight, Sam."

"I'll do that, Miss Pruitt," Sam

answered. "There's a fellow I know; a member of my tribe. People swear he can talk to horses, and they understand him and talk back to him. I'll get him to give Starlight a workout every day, and I'll keep an eye on him."

"That sounds like a wonderful idea, Sam," said Alma, and smiled. "Hope you won't mind having trouble with Miss Decker."

Sam chuckled and his eyes met Alma's. "Having trouble with Miss Decker is an occupational hazard of working at Cypress Groves, Miss Pruitt. I doubt if any of us has escaped the rough side of her tongue from time to time. But we all loved Uncle Dan. We know what he wanted done and, to the best of our ability, we do it, regardless of Miss Decker."

"That's my boy!" Alma beamed at him. "We'd better be getting back, Leona."

"You'll take good care of Mr. Bruce, won't you, Miss Gregory?" Sam asked as he walked with them to the station wagon.

"We all will, Sam—everybody at the hospital. And unless there are some unforeseen complications he ought to be back out here in six or eight weeks. At least that's what we are all hoping," Leona answered.

"That's mighty good news, Miss Gregory. Thanks a lot," said Sam, and stood back as Alma slid beneath the wheel and the station wagon rolled down the drive.

As they came into the county road, Leona realized that Alma was scowling thoughtfully, her hands gripped tightly on the wheel.

"Six or eight weeks," Alma repeated. "You really think it will take that long?"

"Alma, for goodness sake!" Leona protested. "You surely know enough about such accidents to realize that sometimes it takes months, even years, for a patient to recover completely. Bruce will be enormously lucky if he can make it in six or eight weeks."

Alma nodded, still scowling. "I'm just wondering if Sam can keep that tiger kitten from slaughtering Starlight that long."

Startled, Leona gasped, "Oh, surely she wouldn't now, not when she knows Bruce doesn't want Starlight punished."

"Are you kidding?" Alma asked grimly. *"That* one would joyously shoot the horse, if she was a good enough shot to dare; and then look sweetly into Bruce's face and swear she had nothing to do with the death."

"But what could she gain by that?" asked Leona, troubled.

"She would hurt Bruce, because the poor guy really loves that horse and has high hopes for him," Alma answered. "Also, she would have 'avenged' herself on us for what she calls humiliating her in front of Sam."

Leona was wide-eyed, and Alma took one hand from the wheel and patted Leona's clenched hands comfortingly.

"But don't look so distressed, honey," she said quietly. "Now that Sam has been alerted, he'll keep me informed about what she's up to. And if it becomes necessary, I'll 'rustle' the horse and hide him in our barn!"

Leona gasped. "Oh, Alma, you wouldn't," she protested, and added uneasily as Alma glanced at her with an impish grin, *"would you?"*

"With pleasure, and consider it a job well done," Alma said firmly as the station wagon raced in between the tall coquina-rock pillars that marked the entrance to the hospital drive.

Dr. Foster greeted Leona with a look of relief but said nothing about her absence. He walked with her to the recovery room, where they stood beside Bruce's unconscious body for an investigative moment. Then Dr. Foster nodded with satisfaction and drew her to the doorway, where he gave her low-voiced instructions for the care of the patient.

"The next forty-eight hours will be the crucial ones, Nurse," he said formally. "He must not be left alone for a moment. I'll have Cole Jordan standing by in case you need him, and you can send one of the PN's for me if you need me. But I don't think you will."

He seemed to remember the reason she had left the hospital with Alma and turned back to ask, "Did you accomplish the mission for which you went to Cypress Groves?"

"Just in the nick of time, Doctor," Leona explained swiftly. "Orders had been given for the horse to be shot, and the Seminole overseer was armed and ready."

Dr. Foster frowned. "But who would give such an order?"

"Miss Decker," answered Leona as noncommittally as she could.

Dr. Foster's eyebrows went up.

"Well, yes, I suppose she does feel that in his absence she has the right to give orders," he agreed. "But the horse is a very valuable animal. Mr. Pruitt was telling me about him. Surely he's not so vicious he has to be destroyed?"

"Alma insists that he isn't, and the overseer said that in the case of the accident the fault was Bruce's, not Star-light's," Leona explained.

Dr. Foster eyed her with sudden intentness, then went out and left her alone with Bruce. There had been two post-operative patients in the recovery room earlier, but both had now been removed to their rooms and Bruce had the room to himself. Leona stood beside the bed and touched her cold fingers to his wrist. The pulse was surprisingly strong and even; and Bruce seemed to be sleeping soundly.

The door opened behind her and she turned to find Dr. Jordan there. For no reason at all she felt the color rise in her face as Dr. Jordan looked from her down to the unconscious man and a faint smile touched his very good-looking face.

"It won't do you a bit of good, you know," he told her, his tone softly mocking.

"What won't?" Leona asked, not a bit sure that she wanted the question answered.

"Devoting yourself so tenderly to our

wounded hero." Dr. Jordan was still speaking softly, and the mocking note was still in his voice. "Alma's got the Indian sign on him. He's hers, and she could be a pretty deadly enemy if you tried to jump her claim."

"Dr. Jordan, Bruce McClain is my patient, nothing more. He's also your patient and Dr. Foster's."

"True, true." Dr. Jordan was studying the chart, glancing at her now and then beneath his brows. "But Dr. F. and I didn't rush at breakneck speed out to Cypress Groves to save the life of McClain's cherished horse! You and Alma did."

"So what?" Leona's head was up and there was fire in her eyes. "Didn't you hear Bruce tell me as we went into the o.r. that Starlight must not be punished?"

"I'm afraid I didn't. It must have been very touching. I'm sorry I missed it," Dr. Jordan mocked.

Leona looked at him for a long moment, and then she lifted her hands and let them fall in a little gesture of defeat.

"I'd never have suspected it of you," she said quietly, and now it was his turn to be puzzled.

"Suspected what?" he asked.

"That you were insanely jealous of every man in the hospital at whom any woman looks; that you want them all for yourself, just because you are so spectacularly handsome." She stopped, because Dr. Jordan had taken a single step toward her and his hands were on her shoulders, shaking her hard.

"Why, you sassy little so-and-so!" he grated through his clenched teeth, his eyes blazing with anger. "For two cents I'd turn you across my knee and whale the daylights out of you!"

For a moment they glared at each other. And then suddenly Leona laughed. Dr. Jordan's hands fell from her shoulders and bewilderment took the place of the outrage that had been registered in his eyes.

"What's so funny?" he demanded.

Leona was pink with laughter and her eyes were brimming with mirth as she answered. "You are, Dr. Jordan. We both are—standing here beside a patient in dire danger and hurling insults at each other! Conduct, dear Doctor, most unbecoming, unethical and unforgivable in a doctor and a nurse."

For a moment he merely stood and stared at her. And then his jaw hardened and without a word he turned and stalked out of the room.

8

THE first few days were anxious ones. But after Bruce had passed the crisis and his recovery seemed assured, the staff settled down with a long breath of relief. Leona was his special duty nurse, but now and then when it was necessary for her to assist in the o.r., Jane Lester or one of the other RN's took over. At last there was a day when a PN, scared but very anxious to prove her worth, was installed in the room.

Alma was in and out as soon as he was permitted visitors, and she and Leona occasionally had a moment together in the corridor. Alma reported that Starlight was doing fine; that Sam's friend, with the improbable name of Elbert, was training the horse beautifully.

"And how is Carol?" Leona asked after a week or ten days had passed.

"Ever hear of a leopard changing its spots?" Alma asked.

"I've heard it's not considered very practical."

"You've heard right. It's impossible. Carol is Carol," Alma answered. "She's coming to visit Bruce tomorrow. You'd better watch her. I wouldn't trust her around the corner. You'd better not either."

Leona nodded. "I'll keep an eye on her while she's here," she promised.

Alma hesitated, her brows drawn together in a slight frown.

"If only something would happen to make her show her true colors in front of Bruce," she drawled. "But I'm afraid that's too much to hope for. She's a cagey one! I don't think Bruce believes me when I try to warn him against her; and even Gramps isn't sure that I'm not just being spiteful! Men are such fools!"

"I resent that!" said Dr. Jordan, who had just come up behind them.

Alma turned and surveyed him coolly.

147

"Well, you have no business eavesdropping if you don't want to hear unpleasant things about yourself, chum," she drawled.

"Sometimes it's the only way a fellow can really find out just what the gals really think about him," he pointed out.

Alma made a little graceful gesture of dismissal.

"Oh, well, I only spoke about the sex as a general thing," she reminded him sweetly. "I didn't name names, you see."

"And if you had, only McClain's name would have been mentioned, I'm sure," drawled Dr. Jordan.

Leona looked from one to the other, knew they had forgotten her presence and went on her way. She was puzzled. Why should they be displaying such hostility?

Could it possibly be that Dr. Jordan was jealous of Alma's interest in Bruce? That was absurd, Leona told herself, because Dr. Jordan had never, at least in her presence, displayed any genuine interest in Alma.

A good thing for you, my girl, she told herself as she went down to lunch, would be just to mind your own business and concern yourself only with what concerns you. And neither Bruce, Dr. Jordan nor Alma is any concern of yours.

Visiting hours were from two until four in the afternoon. Carol arrived promptly at two, as carefully, as exquisitely dressed as though she expected to step before TV cameras and be seen from coast to coast. Her simple summer frock of printed organdie clung closely to her exquisitely dainty figure. She was hatless, and her silver-gilt curls had been freshly dressed and were held back from her enchanting face with a wide blue ribbon that was exactly the color of her eyes. And the armful of roses and tall spikes of delphinium that she carried was the "calendar girl" touch of perfection.

She greeted Leona curtly and brushed past her into Bruce's room, where she gave a little whimpering cry of distress at sight of him. She dropped the flowers and flung herself upon him, sobbing wildly. Leona caught the look of pain on Bruce's face as the weight of Carol fell on his crushed shoulder, and she moved swiftly to raise the girl.

"Carol, you promised you wouldn't make a scene," Leona told her swiftly as the girl crumpled in her arms, a small, frightened, weeping child.

"Oh, but he looks so *awful!* Oh, Brucie, Brucie darling, I can't bear to see you like this," Carol wailed.

"Oh, for Pete's sake," Bruce was angry and embarrassed, "Carol, mop up! Good grief, I'm fine, or I was until you fell on my bad shoulder!"

"You *are* going to get well, Brucie darling?" Carol whimpered.

"Well, of course he is," Leona snapped.

"And he won't be crippled?" Carol pursued the subject fearfully.

Rage shone in Bruce's eyes and his jaw set hard. But before he could manage an answer, Leona said crisply, "He's going to get well and he certainly is not going to be a cripple. I can't imagine where you ever got that stupid idea."

"But I saw him when that vicious horse

threw him and then kicked him," Carol wailed. "How could he not be crippled?"

"Because Dr. Foster is a very fine surgeon and the operation was a complete success. I really must ask you to leave now, Carol," Leona insisted and guided the unwilling girl to the door. "You are upsetting the patient, and we can't have that. He'll be back at the ranch in a few weeks, and you mustn't worry about him."

"Worry about him?" Carol cried hotly as she stood at the open door, so that Leona could not put her out without a show of force. "I've scarcely slept or eaten since the accident happened. I'm worried *sick* about him!"

"Well, you needn't be," Bruce growled. "I'm doing fine."

Leona got the girl out of the room at last. Once in the corridor, Carol wrenched herself free of Leona and turned on her with blazing eyes.

"You keep your hands off me," she said viciously. "I'll be back tomorrow and every day until he returns to the ranch."

"As long as you behave yourself—" Leona began.

"*Behave* myself?" snapped Carol hotly.

"Such scenes as you've just staged with him are very bad for him."

Carol sneered, "Oh, you'd like it if I pretended I didn't care whether he got well or not, wouldn't you? You've got him here all to yourself and you think you can make a lot of time with him! Well, don't kid yourself. Bruce is *mine*, and neither you nor that Pruitt creep is going to take him away from me."

Leona watched as the girl went swiftly down the stairs. When she went back to her patient, Bruce lay staring out of the window at the brilliant sunlight.

Leona came to the side of the bed and adjusted the bandage that Carol's dramatic onslaught had pushed to one side. When she had finished, he looked up at her gravely.

"I suppose she wants to come back tomorrow?" he asked.

"She assured me she would be here

tomorrow and every day until you are able to return home," Leona told him.

She saw the swift expression of dismay that sped over his face, and then he asked uneasily, "Do I *have* to see her?"

"Not unless you want to."

"Swell! Then don't let her in any more."

Leona laughed. "It's not my place to give such orders," she answered. "You'll have to tell Dr. Foster you don't want to see her, and he'll keep her out."

"Good! He's due pretty soon, isn't he, for afternoon rounds?"

"After visiting hours," Leona answered.

"So if they hang a 'No Visitors' sign on my door, I don't have to have visitors," he said happily, and added as an anxious afterthought, "But that would keep Alma out, too."

"Alma works here, remember?" Leona reminded him with a twinkle.

Bruce looked enormously relieved.

"Oh, yes, that's true," he said happily. "Then she wouldn't have to observe that sign any more than you would, would she?"

"No, of course not."

Bruce beamed. "Then that's swell. Wonderful thing, 'No Visitors' signs. I may plan to have a lot of them printed up to use at the Groves."

"Goodness, you are inhospitable, aren't you?" Leona teased him lightly.

Bruce grinned at her. "Just choosy about my company," he assured her. "And any time you or Alma ever see a sign like that at the Groves, pay it no mind, you hear?"

Leona laughed. "I promise."

Bruce was quiet for a moment while Leona moved unobtrusively about the room bringing it to order.

Bruce watched her as though he liked the look of her smooth movements, and when she caught his eyes, there was a look in them that brought a warm tide of color to her face.

"You told me Starlight was all right, didn't you, Leona?" he asked at last.

"Oh, Alma says he's fine," Leona

154

assured him. "I haven't seen him since the day of the accident, of course."

Bruce's brows drew together in a puzzled frown.

"You saw Starlight the day I came into the hospital?" he asked.

"Yes. Alma and I rode out to be sure he hadn't been hurt," Leona explained.

Bruce sensed something in her manner that he could not quite understand and probed.

"He wasn't hurt?" he asked.

"Why, no, he was fine and fit."

"And Sam's taking good care of him?"

"Well, of course. He has a friend from his tribe who's supposed to be very knowledgeable about horses."

"All Seminoles are, Sam told me."

"And Starlight's being trained and exercised every day. So don't worry about him."

Bruce nodded and relaxed slightly, and his grin was boyish and abashed.

"I suppose you think I'm an awful fool to be so crazy about a horse," he told her awkwardly. "But when I was a kid growing up, I never had a pet. I was always nuts about having a horse," he confessed. "So when I learned there was no mistake and I really had inherited Cypress Groves I bought the finest horse Mr. Pruitt and I could find. Oh, I admit that for a man who can't ride any better than I can, Starlight may have been a bad choice. But you've seen him; isn't he beautiful? I felt when I saw him I *had* to have him. Having him makes up for all the pets I never had as a kid!"

"Then I'm very glad you have him, Bruce. And when you get back to the ranch I'm sure you'll have no trouble at all riding him," Leona told him, touched by his boyish frankness.

"I was so afraid he might have broken a leg or been hurt in some way that would make it necessary to have him shot," Bruce admitted. "I know it sounds silly, but if that had happened—"

"But it didn't, Bruce," Leona assured him, and quailed inwardly at the thought of how nearly it had happened.

"No, praises be, it didn't!" Bruce

beamed happily at her. "When I get back to the Groves, Leona, I want you and Dr. Jordan and Alma to come out for a Sunday afternoon, and we'll get Sam and some of his friends to put on a show for us. They have some very fine horses, and they ride magnificently."

"That sounds like fun," Leona told him.

"And you'll come?" Bruce urged.

"Of course. I'm sure Alma and Dr. Jordan will enjoy it as much as I will."

He studied her for a moment and then he said quietly, "You're very nice, Leona."

Leona twinkled at him demurely.

"Why, thank you!" she said lightly, and added impulsively, "So are you."

Bruce was silent for a moment, and then he chuckled.

"If I had to have an accident, I couldn't have been luckier than to have had it where I could be so well cared for," he told her.

"You really are very lucky," Leona told him, entirely serious now. "Dr. Foster is a very brilliant surgeon and he did a marvelous job. You should be very grateful to him."

"I am," Bruce answered soberly. "And to you, too."

"Oh, I only stood by and handed over the right instruments at the right moment," Leona assured him.

Later, when Dr. Foster arrived for a check-up of the patient's condition, he frowned when he saw the crushed shoulder and the bandage Leona had adjusted. He looked sharply at her and then at Bruce.

"What's this about, Nurse? Has he been giving you trouble?" he demanded brusquely.

"Carol Decker did that," Bruce answered before Leona could. "And if you don't mind, Dr. Foster, I'd like to avoid any further visits from her in the future, at least until I'm able to defend myself."

Dr. Foster scowled.

"You mean she struck you?" he asked.

"She threw herself into his arms,

Doctor," Leona explained demurely. "She was hysterical."

"Oh, she was, was she? Then I can assure you, McClain, she will pay you no more visits," said Dr. Foster.

"I could maybe have a 'No Visitors' sign on my door?" Bruce asked hopefully.

"If you're sure that's what you want," Dr. Foster agreed, and Leona opened the drawer of the small desk beside the door and took out the black and white sign. "I'm surprised Miss Decker has so little self-control. But then I've never noticed that women in love are very self-controlled."

Bruce's white ravaged face colored hotly.

"Oh, she's not in love with me, Dr. Foster," he protested.

"No?" Dr. Foster was deftly replacing the slipped bandage and examining the chart while they talked. "Yet she threw herself upon you and, I dare say, wept? Tears usually go hand in hand with that sort of emotional activity."

"I'd rather not talk about it, Doctor, if you don't mind," said Bruce miserably.

For just a moment there was a twinkle in Dr. Foster's usually stern eyes.

"I don't mind a bit," he drawled. "The one thing I want most of all is to get my surgical nurse back as soon as you can get along without her. There are a couple of operations slated for tomorrow, so I'm afraid you're going to have to accept a substitute for her. One of the PNs, since we can't spare an RN for a patient who is definitely on the mend as you are."

"Hey, that's wonderful news. That I'm on the mend, I mean. How soon can I go home, Doctor?"

"Why; don't you like us here?" Dr. Foster asked. "You've got several more weeks to put up with us, McClain. But you are on the mend, and I couldn't be more pleased. You really *were* a bit of a mess when they brought you in, you know."

"I can imagine," Bruce was apologetic. "And it was all my fault."

"I understand that's quite a horse you

have out there," Dr. Foster suggested as he hung the chart back in place.

"One of the very best, Doctor," Bruce said. "I was just telling Leona that as soon as I get home, I want to have a Sunday afternoon party at the ranch, and I hope you will come, Doctor. I'd be very happy to have you."

"Thanks, that's kind of you," Dr. Foster said. "I hope it can be managed."

He took his leave. When Leona had closed the door behind him and came back to stand beside the bed, Bruce looked up at her with an odd expression as though he had just made a discovery.

"You know, I must have had him pegged all wrong," he admitted. "I'd heard he was strictly a sour-puss and never smiled and had no time for anything except surgery and the mainten-ance of the hospital. Uncle Dan must have liked the guy. He seems quite regular."

"Oh, I'm sure he is," Leona answered brightly, and crossed her fingers in the capacious pocket of her uniform. "But he's terribly busy and over-worked. He just doesn't have time for friendly chit-chat with patients."

Bruce said quietly, "You like him a lot, don't you?"

Leona's eyes flew wide.

"Like him? Well, I don't really know him well enough to be sure," she protested uneasily. "I admire and respect him for his skill and his ability, of course. But Dr. Foster isn't an easy person to know. And you have to know a person fairly well to be sure you like him."

Bruce nodded soberly.

"Then I don't suppose I dare ask you whether you like me," he said after a moment.

Leona's eyes widened and a small smile trembled at the corners of her mouth.

"But I do, Mr. McClain."

"Bruce?" he pleaded.

"All right, Bruce then." Leona smiled at him as she deftly made him more comfortable. "I think you're a very nice person and fun to know and I'm looking forward to that Sunday afternoon at the Groves."

Bruce beamed at her happily.

"Swell!" he said happily. "That gives me something to look forward to. Does that sound corny?"

"Of course not. Flattering!"

"I really mean it," Bruce insisted. "I've never known anybody like you. I guess I've never really had many friends. I've been so busy scrambling to make a living there just didn't seem to be time for friends, or even to be aware that I was lonely. But I think now I must have been don't you?"

"It's quite possible,"Leona answered gently.

"I suppose you've always had a lot of friends, fun and good times? But then you would have, because you are so beautiful," he said wistfully.

Leona laughed. "I'm not at all. It's purely the effect of the uniform and your condition. When people are sick or hurt, a nurse's uniform or a doctor's is just about the most beautiful thing in the world."

Bruce shook his head stubbornly and winced slightly at the pain of the movement.

"It's not that at all," he protested. "I thought so when you were at Palmadora. And you were not in uniform that day."

"Now see here, Bruce," Leona's tone held a touch of authority, "you've talked quite enough for one day. You must rest now if you want to get well and get back home to Starlight."

"Back home to Starlight!" he repeated. "Yes, that's what I want."

"Then you be good now and take a nap. It'll help more than anything," she promised, and smiled down at him before she turned and went quickly out of the room.

9

THE following morning was a busy one, and Leona had no time to think of Carol or even to visit Bruce. There were two operations: one for a burst appendix that the patient had been certain was a tumor that could have been malignant; the other for an abdominal obstruction. And shortly before noon an emergency from the sawmill; a man badly hurt in a fight that had left him with a broken jaw and a fractured leg.

By the time she had finished her duties in the operating room and had changed from surgical garb to a fresh uniform, Leona was sharply aware that she had eaten nothing since an early breakfast.

She was just entering the dining room which was now empty except for one of the circulating nurses who had been on duty with her in the o.r. They smiled wearily at each other but were quite content to eat alone.

Leona was halfway through her meal when Alma, fresh and trim in her aide's uniform, came to the doorway, glanced around and came straight to Leona's table.

"Mind if I join you for a cup of coffee, a cigarette and a smidgin of information?" Alma asked briskly.

"Of course not," Leona answered.

"The information has to do with that sign on Bruce's door. Does that mean he's not doing so well?" asked Alma, trying hard to mask her anxiety with a flippant tone.

Leona explained the reason for the sign, and Alma's eyes widened.

"Whoops!" she gasped when Leona had finished. "Oh, boy, oh, boy! When Carol hears that, I hope I won't be around. The hospital will be shaken to its very foundations! Will she ever be mad!"

"But, Alma, it was Bruce's own request," Leona explained.

"Oh, I believe you, but try to make her

believe it!" Alma said. "Boy, am I ever glad I don't have to be the one to break the news to her! And I hope you won't be, either."

Leona said quietly, "I hope not. But if I am, it is simply a part of my duty as a nurse to protect a patient."

"But when the patient is Bruce McClain, for whom Carol's been sharpening her pretty little claws and whom she intends to marry whether he likes it or not—*ouch!*"

"Bruce explained to Dr. Foster, so it's just barely possible he may tell Carol," Leona said, but there was not too much hope in her voice.

"Barely," Alma agreed. "But I wouldn't bank on it, if I were you."

Leona hesitated and then asked flatly, "Alma, are you in love with Bruce?"

Alma's eyes flew wide in such honest amazement that Leona was answered even before Alma spoke.

"In love with Bruce?" Alma repeated. "Of all the cockeyed ideas! Where the heck did you ever get such a notion?"

"From Dr. Jordan," Leona said. "He thinks you and Carol are rivals and that a marriage between you and Bruce would be a fine thing, since it would merge the two estates."

Alma's expression was so odd that Leona broke off and sat merely staring at her. Alma was amused, triumphant, and something else to which Leona could not quite put a name.

"So the beautiful Cole thinks I'm stuck on Bruce!" Alma mocked. "Well, who'da' thought it?"

"He even indicated he thought *I* might be more than a little interested in Bruce; not merely as a patient but as an attractive man," Leona went on.

Alma chuckled with such obvious delight that Leona was puzzled.

"What's so funny?" she demanded.

Alma grinned impishly. "You wouldn't understand, darling," she cooed sweetly.

"Oh, I'm a big girl now," Leona reminded her. "You'd be surprised how much I can understand."

Alma studied her, a smile curling her lovely mouth, her eyes dancing.

"Oh, well, maybe it wasn't very funny anyway." She stood up. "I'd better get cracking before somebody finds I'm loafing on the job."

"So had I," Leona agreed, and they walked together to the door of the dining room. There Alma laid a swift, restraining hand on her arm and signaled for silence.

Ahead of them in the lobby, Dr. Jordan stood holding a weeping Carol in his arms. Scattered about their feet was a mass of lovely flowers that had spilled from Carol's arms.

Alma swung a glance at Leona and then back to the two before them.

Dr. Jordan was murmuring soothing words to Carol, but Leona and Alma were too far away to distinguish what he was saying. After a moment he guided Carol gently out of the hospital and down the front steps. A moment later they heard the sound of a car starting up, and then Dr. Jordan came back into the lobby.

His jaw was set, and as he saw Alma

and Leona his eyes blazed. For a moment he seemed satisfied just to stand and glare at them accusingly, and then he came striding toward them, the light of battle in his eyes.

"I suppose you two are feeling very proud of yourselves," he accused them, and his voice was low and shaken with fury.

Before Leona could speak, Alma said cooly, *"Et tu, Brute?"*

Dr. Jordan's hands jammed hard into his pockets.

"And what's that supposed to mean?" he demanded.

"If you don't know, why should I explain?" Alma asked sweetly.

"I suppose you're implying that I have been 'taken in' by Carol's wistful appeal?"

"And what else could I mean?" Alma's voice was gentle.

"I don't know why you hate the poor kid so much," he said at last. "She's a lovely girl and has had a rough life, and you seem determined to beat her to a pulp. I can't imagine that it's entirely your battle for Bruce McClain—"

"Well, thanks a heap!"

"Because you displayed your hatred for her long before he ever came here," Dr. Jordan went on as though she had not spoken. "But it seems to me that all these humiliations you've heaped on her are little short of unforgivable. This final one, denying her the right to visit McClain, seems to me the worst yet. It's just about broken the kid's heart."

"It was Bruce's request, Dr. Jordan," Leona said quietly.

Dr. Jordan glared at her, then turned back to Alma.

"I don't believe for a moment that he would ask that visiting privileges be denied her specifically," he snapped, "unless you two put him up to it."

"I had nothing to do with it," Leona said sharply. "Dr. Foster will tell you that."

"Oh, he did," snapped Dr. Jordan, "when he gave me the task of breaking the news to her. Just because he feels I have what he is kind enough to call a 'special talent' for breaking bad news to the families of patients who have died, he seemed to feel this was a job right down my alley. Well, I did it. And I'm not proud of myself—or of either of you."

Leona spluttered indignantly. "I had nothing to do with it."

"Neither did I," said Alma, "but only because I didn't think of it."

For a moment the two glared at each other, and then Dr. Jordan made a small gesture of defeat.

"I don't understand how a girl who has had everything all her life could possibly be so vicious to a kid like Carol," he said wearily.

Alma laughed softly, and the sound was like a blow to Dr. Jordan.

"What you need," he told her very softly, his eyes blazing, "is a good sound spanking!"

"Do tell," Alma mocked. "Oddly enough, that's exactly what Bruce told Gramps not long ago."

"Then he has more sense than I gave him credit for," Dr. Jordan snapped.

"Please don't tell my fiancé that when he comes down next weekend on a visit, will you?" Alma asked him with a pretty pretense of anxiety. "I don't want him to get ideas."

Dr. Jordan looked as though he had taken a step in the dark and discovered the step wasn't there.

"Your fiancé?" he repeated.

"Oh, well, he's not really my fiancé—yet. He has some utterly absurd and ridiculous idea that he can't ask me to marry him until he can support me in the luxury he thinks Gramps has accustomed me to," Alma said cheerfully. "So I've asked him down from Tampa for the weekend so he can see how hard I really work. Then maybe he'll want to take me away from all this—I hope!"

Dr. Jordan looked considerably deflated, and Alma laughed silkily.

"Perhaps you'll come to dinner Saturday night, Cole, and bring Leona. I'd love to have you meet Lance. But please don't suggest you think it would be a good idea for him to beat me! It wouldn't, I can assure you."

They stared at each other for a moment, and then, without a further word, Dr. Jordan turned and strode off down the corridor toward the charity ward.

Paula Ingram was emerging from Dr. Foster's office with a handful of papers. She looked startled and very disapproving as she saw the delphinium and pink roses that Carol had spilled.

"What happened here?" she demanded.

Alma bent swiftly and began gathering up the flowers.

"Miss Decker brought them for Mr. McClain," she explained. "And when she found that Mr. McClain wasn't having visitors, she just dropped them and left."

"Oh," said Paula, "I don't imagine Mr. McClain will want them, since he didn't want to see her. Why not take them to the charity ward, Alma? They'll brighten things up there."

She went on across to her office. When Alma stood up, holding the bright armful, she said to Leona, "It really *is* a shame. Carol must have ordered these from Tampa. They don't grow well here."

Leona nodded soberly. "She brought another armful for him yesterday. Alma, I feel terrible about all this."

Alma nodded thoughtfully. "So do I, honey. But after all, if Bruce insists he doesn't want to see her, there's nothing we can do, is there?"

"No, I suppose not," Leona agreed, and watched as Alma went down the corridor carrying the flowers.

For the next few days the hospital routine, of which Leona was now a well integrated part, went smoothly.

Alma announced blithely on Friday that the dinner party for Saturday night had had to be called off because her Lance could not get away from Tampa. So she was going up to spend the weekend there and would ask Dr. Jordan and Leona to meet him at another time.

Dr. Jordan seemed not at all put out

by the withdrawal of the invitation and simply strode away when Alma told him. She watched him and chuckled as she went outside to the waiting station wagon.

Bruce was now definitely improving, to Dr. Foster's delighted approval. Leona was caught up in the many tasks that fell to the overworked personnel of the hospital and paused only now and then to stop and speak gaily to him before hurrying back to whatever task awaited her.

Therefore when the blow fell it came with such swiftness, such unexpectedness, that it left Leona feeling dazed.

She was called to Dr. Foster's office immediately after lunch one afternoon to find a stout, grizzled-looking middle-aged man sitting beside Dr. Foster's desk, looking very unhappy indeed. He rose as Leona came in and stood turning his broad-brimmed hat uneasily around and around in his big, gnarled-looking hands.

"This is Miss Gregory, Sheriff," said Dr. Foster. And to Leona, his tone hard, he added, "This is Sheriff Wilcox, Leona. He has a warrant for your arrest."

Leona stared wordlessly from one man to the other and then, because her knees would no longer support her, dropped unbidden into a chair.

"A warrant?" she replied incredulously.

"I'm right sorry, Miss Gregory," Sheriff Wilcox told her unhappily. "But when somebody swears out a warrant, it's my job to serve it and to make the arrest."

Leona stammered, "But arrest for what?"

"Horse-stealing," said Sheriff Wilcox.

It seemed to Leona that the floor heaved beneath her and she knew a moment of craziness. She was quite sure she couldn't possibly have heard him correctly and then, suddenly, she knew what was happening.

"A horse named Starlight? From Cypress Groves?" she asked.

Dr. Foster stiffened and the look in his eyes became grim.

Sheriff Wilcox answered, "Then you *did* take the horse, Miss Gregory?"

"Good heavens, no!" Leona protested, and laughed.

"I'm afriad I don't think it's very funny, Miss Gregory," Wilcox said heavily. "The theft of a fine, very valuable horse is no laughing matter."

"Well, of course it isn't, Sheriff," Leona answered quickly. "It's only that it all seemed so utterly crazy! What would *I* want with a horse?"

"Isn't this the horse that sent McClain here?" demanded Dr. Foster.

"Well, yes."

"I believe you and Miss Pruitt were terribly concerned for fear the horse would be destroyed, and you left your patient in the recovery room to go out and check to be sure the horse was safe," said Dr. Foster.

"We did, Doctor, yes," Leona explained, and went on to tell him again how Bruce had pleaded that the horse not be punished.

"And now, Sheriff, the horse is missing?" asked Dr. Foster.

"Miss Decker swore out the warrant, Doctor. Seems she's convinced that Miss Gregory had him stolen or did it herself and has hidden him somewhere," Sheriff Wilcox answered.

"You searched the stables at Cypress Groves?" asked Dr. Foster.

"Well, sure, Doc," Sheriff Wilcox answered. "Not only the stables but the whole place. The Seminole stable hands and that fellow, Sam, that runs the stables, swore that the horse was in his stable last night when they made the rounds. This morning he's gone. And Miss Decker accuses Miss Gregory of stealing him."

Dr. Foster turned to Leona. "Now why should Miss Decker think *you* took the horse, Nurse?" he demanded.

"Honestly, Dr. Foster, I don't know," Leona admitted painfully, "except that she had given orders for Starlight to be shot, and Alma and I arrived just in time to stop Sam from carrying out the order.

179

And Carol was furiously angry and said she'd get even with me. But this whole crazy business is just absurd!"

The two men studied her for a moment. As she had mentioned Alma's name, Leona remembered Alma saying that, if it was necessary to protect Starlight's life, she'd steal him and hide him in her grandfather's stable. Had she?

Sheriff Wilcox said quietly, "You've remembered something, Miss Gregory?"

Leona was very still for a moment, and then she looked up but she could not quite meet the stern gaze of the two men.

"No, nothing. That is, unless you think it's possible Carol could have had the horse shot and now wants to pretend it's been stolen?" she offered uneasily.

"Not a chance of that, Miss Gregory." Sheriff Wilcox shook his graying, partially bald head. "Sam is a man whose word I'd take on oath or even without it. He assures me that the horse, was in his stable last night. If Miss Decker had shot the horse, how could she have disposed of the body, alone and unaided?"

"Well, for that matter, how could *I* have gotten him away from the Groves?" Leona asked.

"By riding him, of course. That's a silly question."

"But I *can't* ride, and Starlight was a very mettlesome beast."

"Why do you say 'was', Miss Gregory? Is the horse dead?"

"Goodness, how should I know?" Leona protested. "I haven't seen the horse since the day Bruce was thrown. The last thing on earth I would have done was to steal him."

Sheriff Wilcox glanced at Dr. Foster.

"I sure hate to do this, Doc," he said heavily, "but I'll have to place her under arrest."

"Yes, of course, I quite see that," Dr. Foster agreed, and his face was set in lines so stern that Leona felt she was seeing the man for the first time.

"You can pack a bag if you like, Miss Gregory."

There was a knock at the door, and before anybody could speak, it was thrust open and Lamar Pruitt came striding in, his face a dark thundercloud.

"What in tarnation's going on here?" he demanded sharply. "Wilcox, what are you up to? Foster, why are you letting him get away with it? Leona, honey, tell me about it. Arresting you for rustling, are they? Well, we'll just see about that. Rustling, my left-hand foot!"

Leona felt tears prick her eyelids, but she managed a smile.

"They think I stole Starlight," she told him.

"That's what Sam said when he called me. Said that Decker gal had sworn out a warrant. Of all the fool—" He turned sharply to the sheriff. "I'll make bond for the girl, Wilcox. Now you get travelin' and find that horse."

"That's what I aim to do, Mr. Pruitt," said Sheriff Wilcox. "And if you're going to make bond for the girl, you come along with me and let's get it tended to. I don't want to arrest her, but if I have to, I'll do it."

"You try it, Wilcox, and see where it

gets you," snapped Lamar, and patted Leona warmly on the shoulder. "I'll be right back, honey. You keep your chin up."

"Thanks—oh, Mr. Pruitt, thanks!" Leona said, and a tear slid from her eyes despite her efforts to control her emotions.

When the door had closed behind the two men, Dr. Foster scowled at Leona, deeply troubled rather than annoyed.

"I can't understand why Carol Decker should do such a thing," he said. "It seems ridiculous on the face of it. Of course you know that it's going to be very unpleasant before it's finished."

"I know," Leona said huskily. "She was so angry when Alma and I stopped her from destroying the horse. And she said then that she would get even with me. She even went so far as to say she'd make the hospital much too hot to hold me."

Dr. Foster nodded. "I can see that's what she's trying to do. There will be newspaper items about this. The wire services will pick it up. They'll handle it facetiously, of course. I can imagine the headlines: 'Nurse Rustles Race Horse,' or some such nonsense. It's pure vindictiveness on Carol's part. But I'm surprised she'd go to such lengths just to get rid of you."

"Being denied visiting privileges to Bruce just about put the finishing touches on her hatred for me, Dr. Foster," Leona pointed out.

"But that was by his own request. Surely she can't hold you responsible for that?" he protested.

"I'm sure she does, Dr. Foster. So I think the best thing I can do, for the hospital's sake, is to ask for a release from my contract so that I can leave immdiately."

Dr. Foster said sharply, "Oh, come now. I have no intention of allowing Carol Decker to tell me how to run this place. I need you here. You're a fine nurse."

"That's very kind of you, Doctor," Leona told him evenly. "But with Carol hating me as she does and as vindictive as she obviously is, I feel sure that she will continue to harass me *and* the hospital as long as I am here. So I think I'd better go. That is, if I'm allowed to."

"Oh, you mean the warrant? Pruitt will make bond. But I don't suppose you will be allowed to leave town until after the trial," Dr. Foster told her.

Leona caught her breath and her eyes flew wide.

"There will be a trial?" she asked.

"Well, of course." Dr. Foster seemed astonished that she had not expected that.

Leona drew a deep breath and made a little gesture of defeat.

"I should have known that," she admitted, and managed a sorry attempt at a smile. "It's just that I've never been arrested before."

Dr. Foster said something savage under his breath.

"And you shouldn't be now," he said when he had his temper somewhat under control. "In fact, you could probably sue Carol Decker for slander or false arrest or something."

Leona managed a ghost of a smile as she stood up and found to her surprise that her knees would now support her.

"The thought isn't very appealing," she said. "I'll just be glad when the trial can be finished and I can get away. And I do hope that the hospital need not get involved in unpleasant publicity just because I've worked here."

"The hospital can survive anything but a suit for malpractice," Dr. Foster assured her.

"And that's something that could never, never happen here, Dr. Foster," Leona answered earnestly. "I've been here long enough to know how impossible that would be."

Dr. Foster smiled at that, but his eyes were still troubled.

"I'd say no more impossible than having one of my nurses charged with stealing a horse!" he told her, and Leona managed a faint chuckle.

"Well, thanks a lot, Dr. Foster," she told him. "I've liked working here and I shall hate to leave. But I feel it's best all around. As long as Carol is so near at hand, and her enmity is so vicious, there's no knowing what she may do next to be rid of me."

She said good night to him and went up to her own room.

She put the light on and brought out her suitcase and began packing. The sooner she could get away the better. She would have to manage some sort of goodbye to Bruce; some way that would not indicate to him that Carol had had any hand in her leaving. In the meantime, she could not but wonder what Carol had done with Starlight.

10

LEONA was so accustomed to the sounds of the hospital that she scarcely noticed them. The ringing of bells; the swift movement of feet in the corridors; low voices; even a light tap at her door scarcely penetrated her unhappy absorption until it was repeated and she opened the door to a Seminole PN whose eyes widened as she saw the evidence of packing in the room.

"Miss Gregory, Dr. Jordan would like you to come to the recovery room right away, please."

Leona thanked her, pulled the door shut and hurried to the recovery room, where Dr. Jordan stood beside a patient who had just been brought from the operating room. There was an anxious, troubled look in his eyes as he glanced at Leona and then once more at the patient.

"Where were you while the operation

was going on, Leona?" he asked curtly. "Why was Miss Ingram on duty?"

Before she could answer he went on, "This patient is going to need special duty, and since you're our best, I'd like you to be in charge."

Conscious of the nurse who stood beside the plasma kit, watching as the life-giving fluid dripped bit by slow bit into the patient's veins, Leona said under her breath, "I'm sorry, Dr. Jordan. I can't. I'm leaving."

Dr. Jordan straightened as though she had slapped him, and his brows drew together in a puzzled, angry scowl. He glanced at the nurse and gave her a low-toned order. Then with his hand under Leona's elbow, he guided her out of the room and into the corridor.

"What the devil do you mean you're leaving?" he demanded sharply.

"Just that," she told him levelly. "There's no secret about it. At least there won't be for long. I'm about to be arrested on a warrant sworn out by Carol Decker."

Dr. Jordan obviously thought she was making it up and gave her a little shake.

"Cut out the nonsense and talk sense," he demanded. "If you've fought with Foster—"

"I haven't," Leona assured him, and went on to tell him about the warrant. "So for the good of the hospital, to keep them from being involved, I'm resigning."

Dr. Jordan stared at her as though he had never heard such a ridiculous story.

"But that's fantastic," he protested. "Why should Carol Decker want you arrested?"

"She's accusing me of stealing the McClain horse, Starlight," Leona told him.

Dr. Jordan said after a long moment. "Now I've heard everything!"

"I feel the same way," Leona answered frankly. "But the sheriff is taking it quite seriously. He obviously sees nothing funny about the charge. In fact, I'm not sure he believes I'm not guilty."

"We'll see McClain about this," said

Dr. Jordan grimly but Leona drew back, shaking her head.

"We'll do nothing of the sort," she protested. "He's in no condition to be upset by anything so silly. Starlight *is* missing, and that would distress him."

"Having you arrested, charged with stealing the brute, wouldn't upset him, I suppose?" Dr. Jordan grated between his teeth.

"Why should it?" Leona asked quietly. "He's crazy about Starlight, who represents to him all the things he wanted and didn't have when he was a boy. I'm just a nurse who has tended him."

"A nurse who is desperately in love with him," Dr. Jordan said and Leona caught her breath and looked up at him, suddenly realizing that he had read her heart better than she herself.

"Oh, golly," she wailed, "is it as obvious as all that?"

Dr. Jordan's smile was faint, and there was more than a touch of bitterness in it.

"Only to someone else as desperately

and even more hopelessly in love as you are," he answered.

Leona met his eyes.

"It's Alma, isn't it?" she asked with a flash of intuition.

Dr. Jordan nodded.

"Can you imagine anything more hopeless than that?" he asked heavily. "She knows I'm alive, because I squirm when she sticks shafts of ridicule in me. But I amuse her, that's all. And even if by some incredible miracle she *should* decide I might be a man she could love, what chance would I have? The daughter of Palmadora, and a penniless guy just getting ready to hang out his shingle and starve for a few years until he can build up a practice?"

"Poor Alma," said Leona after a moment of silent thought.

"Poor Alma?" Dr. Jordan repeated.

"Well, the man she wants to be her fiancé is a young lawyer in Tampa, who's just starting out. And he won't marry her or even be engaged to her until he's making a lot of money. And now you feel

192

you shouldn't let her know you love her because *you're* just starting out! So—poor Alma!"

Dr. Jordan's handsome face was touched with a cynical smile.

"Well, there's Bruce McClain, worth millions and with an estate that adjoins hers. I'm sure he's hers for the taking any time she wants to lift her little finger," he pointed out.

"And there's Carol standing by ready to do some devilish thing to prevent that from happening," Leona reminded him.

"Oh, yes, Carol," said Dr. Jordan as though he had just that moment remembered her. "We'll have to do something about Carol, won't we?"

"I'm getting as far away from her as I can," Leona answered and the door behind her opened as the nurse summoned Dr. Jordan swiftly to his patient.

All Leona's professional instincts, her training, her skill and her warm desire to be of service urged her to follow Dr. Jordan and to do what she could to help.

But the patient would need a special duty nurse who could be with her as long as she was needed. And for the good of the hospital Leona had to go away.

She started back to her own room, and then she looked across the corridor to the door of Bruce's room. She stood hesitant for a moment, and then she realized that she could not leave the hospital without saying goodbye to him.

She opened the door very cautiously but Bruce was propped up against his pillows reading; not asleep as she had thought he might be.

He greeted her with such warm delight that her heart turned over in her breast and a warm tide of color rose in her face.

"Hey, you've been neglecting me," he accused her. "I could have lain here and died for all the attention you gave me!"

Leona laughed and made a pretense of examining the chart at the foot of his bed.

"Oh, you wouldn't do a dirty trick like that after we've all worked so hard to make you live," she mocked him. "I've been terribly busy, and you should be glad you no longer need a special. That means you're well on the road to recovery, you know. First thing you know you'll be back at the Groves and having a wonderful time."

He nodded happily. "I just hope that friend of Sam's has been taking good care of Starlight," he said lightly, and added, like an abashed small boy, "I know you think I'm a fool to be so crazy about that horse."

"I don't at all," Leona answered, and kept a careful rein on both her voice and her expression. "I understand how much he means to you."

"Thanks," said Bruce gratefully. "There's only one thing I'll hate about getting back to the Groves. That's not being able to see you every day."

"Oh, but even if you decided to make your home here in the hospital you wouldn't see me every day," Leona reminded him.

"I could raise such a ruckus you'd have to come and see me at least once a day if I lived here," he told her firmly.

"But, you see, I won't be here after today," Leona said, and had a moment's pride that her voice sounded so casual, so matter of fact.

Bruce stared at her, shocked.

"You're leaving the hospital?" he asked.

"Tomorrow morning," Leona said quietly.

"But why? Don't you like it here? Everybody seems crazy about you."

"Thanks." Leona smiled. "Yes, I like it here. But I'm going back to Atlanta to work with my father in his office."

Even as she said it she marveled that, without in the least being conscious of such a thought, she had reached that decision. Her father would be overjoyed; and she and Irene would be friends!

She was startled at the look of despair that touched Bruce's face.

"I should have known I'd lose you," he said huskily, "just as, all my life, I've always lost everything that I wanted most. I suppose that's why Starlight means so much to me. He, at least, is one thing I wanted desperately and got."

Leona caught her breath on a small soundless gasp. And now Starlight had slipped away from him!

Bruce was following his own train of unhappy thought and was quite unaware of her gasp. He was studying her now with a look of sad intensity and made a slight gesture with his uninjured hand.

"I knew, of course," his smile was faint and mirthless, "that I was being a colossal fool to fall in love with you in the beginning. I tried to talk myself out of it that afternoon when I met you for the first time. But the more I tried, the harder I fell. So of course I knew you'd go away and I'd never see you again."

Leona was staring at him with enormous, incredulous eyes.

"Are you trying to tell me that you love me?" she asked incredulously.

"Well, of course." Bruce seemed surprised that she had not guessed. "I'm making a miserable business of it, of course. Only it's the first time I've ever been really in love, and it's hard to find the right words, especially now when you've just told me you're leaving."

"But I thought you and Alma—" Leona said faintly.

Once more he made a slight gesture as if he brushed away a cobweb.

"Oh, Alma and I are pals," he admitted. "We kid around a lot. But you don't kid around with a girl when you're in love with her. At least I don't."

Leona stood looking down at him, her hands jammed into the pockets of her uniform. Something in her eyes made him struggle to raise himself a little from his pillows; and automatically her nurse's training made her put her hands on his shoulders and push him gently back. His uninjured hand reached for hers and closed tightly about it.

"If I come to Atlanta one of these days, Leona, would you give me a date?" he asked eagerly.

Leona laughed softly, but it was a laugh caught with tears.

"Yes blessed idiot!" she said softly. "If

you want me to stay here, I won't even go to Atlanta. Bruce, don't you know that I am in love with you?"

Bruce gasped, "Oh, but you can't be! Not a bungling no-good like me! Not when there's a handsome guy like Cole Jordan around."

"Oh, Bruce, Bruce, darling." Leona bent her head and set her mouth on his, and for a stunned moment Bruce lay very still, just looking at her, his eyes wide with wonder.

"Leona?" he whispered at last, as though he were caught in some glorious spell that the smallest wound might shatter.

"Yes, darling?" Leona said softly, and smiled tenderly down at him.

"Is this for real? You aren't just kidding?" he pleaded for reassurance.

"Would I, darling, about this?" she asked tenderly.

"I can't believe it," he said at last.

"Bruce dearest," she told him tenderly, "it's the most wonderful thing that ever happened to me, too. I was so sure that you and Alma were in love."

"Oh that! She was just trying to help me escape Carol." He grinned and instantly sobered, "That's a pretty nasty thing to say about the poor kid, I know."

Leona straightened and her jaw set.

"It isn't half nasty enough," she said, and was ashamed of herself. "Bruce darling, I have to tell you something. Promise you won't get upset?"

"Not unless you're going to tell me you've made a mistake about being in love with me."

"That I'll never do," Leona assured him firmly.

"And you'll marry me?" His tone was fearful.

"The very minute you leave the hospital," she promised.

"Then you can tell me anything you want to tell me and I promise I won't get upset," he assured her happily.

Still Leona hesitated.

"It must be something pretty terrible if you're afraid to tell me," Bruce said at last. "Unless you're going to tell me you're already married—"

"Oh, darling, that's utter nonsense," Leona told him, and went on quietly, "Starlight is missing."

For a moment he just went on looking up at her, scowling as though he didn't quite know what she was talking about. And then what she had said registered and she saw the faint shock.

"Well, of course," he said heavily at last.

Startled, Leona gasped, "You knew?"

"Only that if I was going to have you, which is a blessed miracle, I couldn't have my horse as well," he told her. "A fellow never gets two such miracles."

"Bruce, you're delirious," Leona protested.

"Sure am," he agreed happily. "Delirious with joy. Well, go ahead and tell me. What happened to Starlight?"

"Nobody seems to know," Leona admitted. "Carol has sworn out a warrant for my arrest for stealing him."

And now the shock she had been

braced to see on his face was there; shock and incredulity and a slowly dawning fury as he realized that she was telling him the truth.

"Carol dared to do that to you?" he asked. His tone was savage with anger, and once more she had to force him back against his pillows, for he was determined to get up despite his weakness.

"You promised you wouldn't be upset, darling," Leona pleaded with him. "Perhaps I shouldn't have told you until you are able to be up and around. But, Bruce, I felt you had to know and that maybe it would be better for me to tell you than to have you hear it from someone else. The news is all over the hospital by now; you could hear a garbled account."

Bruce was swearing half under his breath and Leona's eyes widened a little at the color and the variety of his profanity. Gradually he subsided against his pillows.

"That she should dare!" he whispered. And then to Leona, "I want to see my lawyer, immediately. Have him come here at once."

Leona smothered a soft laugh against his angry mouth.

"Oh dearest, I don't need a lawyer," she laughed tenderly. "Mr. Pruit is making bond for me so that I won't have to go to jail. And when the case is set for trial there will be plenty of time to find a lawyer for me."

"You'll never come to trial and there'll be no jail," said Bruce savagely. "I want to see my lawyer to file suit against Carol."

"Now that's silly, darling," Leona soothed him. "To try to fight the case, or to file a suit against her—why, that would just make things worse."

"I'm not thinking of filing a case against her," said Bruce harshly. "I'm thinking of filing an eviction notice against her. I want her out of my house and out of the state just as fast as she can travel. I've put up with a lot of nonsense from her. Her mother is a very decent sort. But this action puts Carol completely beyond any compassion I might once have felt for her. Uncle Dan left them a nice trust fund. I'll add to it or give them a check for a year's expenses. But I want them out and away by the end of the week! My lawyer will know how to handle it, since you won't let me go out there and forcibly throw them out personally."

"Now, now, now," Leona soothed him tenderly, "you promised not to get upset."

"You expect me not to when the girl I love is being badgered by that—that—" He strangled on the epithet, and Leona winced, but there was a twinkle in her eyes.

"You promised," she reminded him. "And if you go getting upset and struggling and fighting, you're going to be here in the hospital a long, long time. Is that what you want?"

"You know I don't," he told her huskily.

"Good! Then you'll behave?"

"If you'll have my lawyer come here,"

Bruce bargained. "He is Arthur Rowley, and his number is in the phone book."

"And I'm sure he'll be here as fast as I can call him," Leona soothed him.

There was a light tap at the door, and it opened to admit one of the PNs who announced, "There are some people to see you, Miss Gregory. They are in the lobby."

"One of them wouldn't be Carol Decker?" demanded Bruce sharply.

The PN grinned impishly.

"Oh, no, Mr. McClain. They're strangers, and they seem very anxious to see Miss Gregory," she answered.

"You stay here, Eleanor, and keep an eye on Mr. McClain," ordered Leona. "He seems to be very restless and to have a great desire to get out of bed, and that we can't allow yet a while."

"Oh, my goodness no, Miss Gregory." The PN was shocked at the bare idea.

Leona grinned impishly down at Bruce and said, "Now, let's see you try any foolishness. Eleanor is a Seminole, and I understand that she's quite strong."

The PN laughed. "I wouldn't have a job here if I couldn't handle patients like Mr. McClain," she said, and Bruce groaned at the conspiratorial glance that passed between the two women.

11

THERE was no one in the lobby except the personnel Leona had expected to see there, and she crossed to the switchboard and put her question.

"Oh, yes, Miss Gregory. They were asking for you, and then Dr. Foster came up the corridor and took them into his office. You're to go right in," announced the pretty copper-skinned girl in charge of the switchboard.

Leona tapped lightly at the closed door of Dr. Foster's office and heard his voice calling, "Come in." She swung the door open, her heart beating a little faster, the faintest possible feather edge of uneasiness brushing her.

But the opened door revealed to her the last two people in the world she had expected to see: her father and Irene.

For a dazed instant she stood staring

from her father's anxious, concerned face to Irene's, that was no less strained. And then she cried out, "What are you two doing here, for goodness sake!"

"What are we doing here?" Dr. Gregory was embracing her warmly, while Irene looked on. "You must surely have known we'd get here as fast as we could when we received your wire."

Leona's eyes widened and she gasped, "My wire? But I didn't send you a wire!"

Dr. Gregory drew a flimsy yellow slip from his pocket, and Leona looked down at it and read the message. "Please come immediately. In desperate trouble. Leona."

Leona stared from the message to her father and then at Dr. Foster.

"The Decker girl again?" asked Dr. Foster, but his tone made it a statement, not a question.

"It must be her work," Leona glanced again at the telegram and added swiftly, "It was sent this morning! And I didn't even know about the warrant until after lunch."

Dr. Gregory's brows drew together in an angry scowl.

"Warrant? What warrant?" he demanded.

"You haven't told them, Dr. Foster?" Leona asked.

"There hasn't been time. They have only just arrived," he answered.

"Well, somebody better get started telling me what this is all about, and fast! I'm not a patient man," Dr. Gregory barked sharply.

"Now, Amos dear, Leona will tell you," Irene soothed him anxiously.

"There's a warrant out for my arrest for stealing a horse, Daddy," said Leona demurely, and saw her father's face take on an all but apopletic hue. "Only it's really just a gag, I suppose. I mean, the girl who did it was just trying to get rid of me, because she wants the man I'm going to marry."

Dr. Foster's eyebrows shot up at that, but Dr. Gregory simply waited. As swiftly as she could Leona gave them a run-down on what had happened. By the time she had finished, Dr. Gregory could not quite make up his mind whether to go into a towering rage at the insult to his daughter or to consider the whole thing a cruel joke of monumental proportions.

Then he asked, "And what's this about this gal wanting the man you're going to marry? This is the first I've heard of you planning to marry anybody. Who is he?"

Leona glanced at Dr. Foster. Her color was high and there was a warm sweetness in her eyes as she told her father of Bruce and how they had met.

"He's here in the hospital? Then I want to meet him. I'm not a bit sure I'm going to give my consent. It's only fair to warn you, girl," said Dr. Gregory sternly.

"Oh, you'll like him, Dad! He's a pretty wonderful person!"

"Oh, is he? Well, I'm not a daft young girl madly in love with some young scalawag, so I'll judge him for myself," growled Dr. Gregory.

"Now, Amos," said Irene gently, and there was a twinkle in her eyes as she winked at Leona. "Your daughter is not a daft young girl. She's a mature, sensible young woman, and I'm quite sure she is an excellent judge of character. And don't you dare tell me to keep out of this, for I have no intention of standing by and letting you make difficulties for Leona and her boy friend."

They were moving toward the door when it opened without the preliminary of a knock and Lamar Pruitt came in. He pulled up short as he saw the two strangers and then addressed Dr. Foster, "Well, it's all attended to. We couldn't get the warrant withdrawn. That Decker girl's got a whim of iron. I have never wanted so much to wallop a woman in my life. I guess maybe it's just as well Sheriff Wilcox was with me or I'm not sure I would have been responsible for what I might have done."

"Mr. Pruitt, I'd like you to meet my father, Dr. Amos Gregory," said Leona, and reached out her hand for Irene, who looked mildly surprised and then beamed as she put her hand in Leona's and let herself be drawn forward. "And my mother, Mr. Pruitt," said Leona, her voice soft and warm as she caught the glint of tears in Irene's lovely eyes.

"Well, now, this is great." Lamar shook hands happily with both of them. "Leona here needed some of her family with her. Not but what Alma and I were ready to fight for her any time she needed it, but this is an ugly business. But Leona won't be arrested. I've made bond for her."

"That's mighty decent of you, sir," said Dr. Gregory. "I'll relieve you of that burden now that I'm here."

"Oh, you will, will you?" Lamar bristled indignantly. "Well, I'd just like to see you try it. This is quite a girl you've got here, Doctor. And she saved my life. Oh, you and Jordan helped, Dr. Foster, I admit—but in the long pull towards convalescence, it was Leona that did the job. Phlebitis, Dr. Gregory. A phlebotomy, as I'm sure you're aware, is no Sunday school picnic."

Gravely Dr. Gregory said, "It truly isn't, Mr. Pruitt. I congratulate you on your recovery. But this bond you have made for my daughter is really my responsibility—"

Leona, eyes twinkling, said demurely, "Now, boys, don't fight! I accept the bond you made for me, Mr. Pruitt, and thanks a million. And as for you, Dad, you just hang onto that amount, and maybe I'll let you spend it on my wedding."

Lamar's bushy eyebrows went up.

"That something that's going to happen soon?" he asked with eager interest. "So you and Cole Jordan are making a match of it, just as I felt you would from the first."

Leona's color burned hotly, but she said steadily, "I'm going to marry Bruce McClain, Mr. Pruitt. There was never any thought of my marrying Cole Jordan."

Lamar's bushy eyebrows shot up.

"Oho!" he said. "So now I begin to understand the motive behind Carol's attack on you! She thought she had Bruce all roped and branded with her name."

"She didn't," Leona said a trifle smugly. "I thought Alma had, but then she told us about the man in Tampa."

Dr. Gregory looked from one to the other with an expression of complete exasperation.

"So you understand, do you, Pruitt? How about you, Dr. Foster? Do you understand, too?" he demanded.

Dr. Foster smiled, and once again Leona was startled at the change the smile made in his usually stern face.

"How could I possibly? I only work here," he drawled.

Leona turned to her father, tucked her hand through his arm and her other hand through Irene's, and looked beseechingly at Dr. Foster.

"May I take Dad and Mother up to meet Bruce?" she asked.

"I see no reason why not," Dr. Foster answered, but added warningly, "He must not be told about the Decker girl's activities or that this horse is still missing."

"He already knows, Dr. Foster," Leona said quietly, "I told him."

Dr. Foster asked sharply, "How did he take it?"

"Well, he was very angry, of course. And he wants his attorney to come here to see him as quickly as possible. He's got a job he wants the attorney to attend to," Leona answered, awkwardly.

"That would be Arthur Rowley," said Lamar, and nodded. "I've got a pretty good picture of what Bruce wants with him, and I'll get in touch with him immediately."

"Oh, would you, Mr. Pruitt? Thanks an awful lot," said Leona gratefully. And to her father, "Now come along, you and Irene, and meet your future son-in-law."

"That's quite a girl, Dr. Gregory," said Lamar as he held the door open for them.

"We like her," said Dr. Gregory with a beaming smile that added great emphasis to the simple words. "Don't we, Irene?"

"We adore her," Irene said swiftly.

At the door of Bruce's room, Leona turned to her father.

"Now don't you go roaring and scaring him off," she warned. "I love him and I intend to marry him, and I don't want him to be afraid of you."

"I resent that!" her father said sternly.

"You shouldn't, darling," said Irene sweetly, "because you *do* go around roaring and yelling when you're cross with somebody."

"Did I ever roar at you?" demanded Dr. Gregory.

"Of course not, darling. And I wouldn't have been afraid of you if you had," Irene assured him serenely, and Leona saw how her father's expression softened as he looked down at the lovely woman who was his wife.

Leona swung open the door, and Bruce turned his head eagerly to welcome her. His eyes widened slightly as he saw Dr. Gregory and Irene. Leona went over to stand beside his bed, aligning herself with him as her hand slid into his and she faced the other two.

216

"Darling, I want you to meet my parents," said Leona, and there was warmth and tenderness and a vast pride in her voice. "Dad, Irene, this is Bruce. I'm not going to ask you to try to like him, because once you get to know him you won't be able not to like him. And, Bruce, you must like them too, so we can all be a family."

Dr. Gregory was studying Bruce with a sharp scrutiny. There was, Leona was secretly amused to notice, something approaching professional interest in Dr. Gregory's eyes as he studied Bruce. Suddenly she chuckled.

"If you'd like to look at the chart, Dad darling, it's there at the foot of the bed," she said gently, her eyes mocking. "But I do assure you Bruce has had the finest medical attention and within another month is going to be as good as new."

"Don't be impertinent," Dr. Gregory tried to scold her even as he took the chart and moved to a window with it, while Irene smiled and chatted with Bruce.

"This is a wonderful surprise, meeting you two like this," Bruce told her, "though I admit I'd like it even better if I was up and on my feet. I feel such a fool lying here being congratulated on the most incredible luck any man could ever have: finding a girl like Leona who is willing to marry me."

Dr. Gregory hung the chart back at the foot of the bed and stood there with his hands jammed into his pants pockets, his eyes fastened on Bruce.

"Well, as long as you realize your luck, young man," he said, with a pretense of sternness.

"Oh, believe me, sir, I do," Bruce insisted. "I've known since the first day I saw her that more than anything in the world I wanted her to marry me. But I found it hard to believe that I was going to be that lucky. There's a certain male charmer on the staff here, name of Dr. Jordan, who has given me some pretty bad moments."

"Oh, darling, don't be silly," Leona protested. "Dr. Jordan is not and never has been interested in me. There's someone else for him."

"Then he's not as smart as I've been giving him credit for being," said Bruce firmly.

Dr. Gregory's trained eyes saw the signs of a patient who was growing weary, and he made a move to leave the room.

"I'll probably see you again before I return to Atlanta," he said as he ushered the two women toward the door.

"Please do, sir. We haven't had a chance really to talk," Bruce pleaded, and added with that boyishness Leona found so endearing, "Give me a good thought to sleep on, Doctor. Tell me, at least, that you aren't going to object to her marrying me."

Dr. Gregory's eyebrows went up slightly.

"You mean am I going to forbid the banns?" he asked.

Bruce grinned ruefully. "Well, I suppose I did mean something like that, sir."

"Well, for your information, young

man, I have no such intention," Dr. Gregory told him and added firmly, "But if you know her well enough to want to marry her as you say you do, you certainly ought to know that if she wants to marry you, and she says she does, nothing I can do or say will stop her. I'll see you in the morning, if Dr. Foster will permit it."

At the door Leona looked back at Bruce; and then suddenly she moved swiftly back across the room and bent to kiss him. Then she was gone and the door had closed behind her.

In the lobby they found Lamar and Dr. Foster in earnest conversation. As they approached, Lamar came to meet them.

"Rowley will be here at eight, and Dr. Foster says it will be all right for him to see Bruce briefly," he announced happily. "And you are all coming to Palmadora with me for dinner. Dr. Gregory, I want you and Mrs. Gregory to be house guests at Palmadora for as long as you can stay. There's some fine fishing."

Dr. Gregory held up a protesting hand even as he grinned wistfully.

"Let me take a rain check on that if I may, Mr. Pruitt, and don't tempt me beyond my strength," he pleaded humorously. "I have to be back in Atlanta in time for office hours on Monday."

"Oh, I'm disappointed," protested Lamar sincerely. "But you will come again soon. And anyway, you three are coming home for dinner with me tonight. It's all settled."

Leona looked beyond him to Dr. Foster and asked, "May I?"

Dr. Foster reminded her. "If you'll withdraw your resignation and stay on with us."

"Oh, I'd love to," Leona assured him, and added with a blush, "For a while."

"That's all we could expect under the circumstances." Dr. Foster once more gave her that faint smile to which his tired, stern face was so accustomed.

"Irene, come up with me while I change," Leona invited, and added to the men, "We won't be long."

As they mounted the wide stairs, Leona explained eagerly, "There are ramps, of course, for the patients who require them. But for a building only two stories high an elevator would be silly."

At the top of the stairs, as she turned toward the corridor that led to the nurses' quarters, Leona saw Dr. Jordan coming from the other direction and paused to wait for him, saying to Irene, "Here's someone you must meet." And to Dr. Jordan, "I'd like you to meet my mother, Mrs. Gregory."

"An unexpected and delightful pleasure, Mrs. Gregory," said Dr. Jordan. And to Leona, his brows drawn together, "You sent for them? You were that worried about Carol's shenanigans?"

"It was Carol who sent them a wire, signing my name and saying I was in trouble," Leona explained.

Dr. Jordan's scowl deepened.

"That one doesn't overlook a bet, does she?" he muttered. And then with a charming smile to Irene, he excused himself and went his way.

"What a perfectly charming man," said Irene as she followed Leona into her small but quite cheerful room.

"He is, isn't he?" Leona agreed gaily. "He's the beau ideal of the whole staff."

"That I can easily imagine," said Irene, glancing about the small room appraisingly.

"I have to admit it's not a penthouse at the Ritz." Leona laughed. "But I spend very little time in it, and the bed is quite comfortable."

She turned to the narrow shallow closet, and Irene stood for a moment watching her before she said quietly, "Leona, I have to ask you something."

Leona turned, holding across her arm the thin pale green cotton dress she planned to wear to dinner.

"Yes, Irene?"

"When you left Atlanta you made it distressingly plain that you hated me," said Irene after a moment. "It hurt badly; and I was prepared to have more of the same treatment from you when Amos and I arrived here. Instead you've introduced me as your mother; you've been very sweet and have almost made me believe that we may some day be friends."

There was a mist of tears in Leona's eyes and her smile was warm if somewhat tremulous.

"It's very simple, darling," she said gently. "I fell in love with Bruce. I didn't especially want to; it was just one of those things that come out of the blue, like a flash of lightning. And then I realized that must be the way you felt about Dad, the way he felt about you. Suddenly I could see what a filthy little beast I'd been. I'm terribly sorry, Irene. Can you ever forgive me? Mind you, I won't blame you if you can't."

"Oh, will you hush?" Irene's voice shook slightly as she put her arms about Leona and drew her close. "Honey, if you could ever imagine what it meant to me that you and I can at last be friends!"

"You're sweet, Irene." Leona was smiling, though her voice was far from steady. "I don't wonder Dad's crazy about you. I just hope Bruce and I will always be as much in love as you two are."

"If there's any doubt in your mind about that, darling, then you mustn't marry the man," Irene told her swiftly. "It's the only thing that makes marriage worthwhile. Without it—well, without it there just isn't any point at all."

Leona hugged her and laughed joyously.

"Oh, I'm sure, darling. I'm very, very sure," she boasted happily.

"Then that's all that matters," said Irene. "Now hurry and get dressed, honey. Frankly, I'm starving. We were much too upset about you to eat on the plane."

And the two who had once been enemies smiled warmly at each other, held snugly in the circle of a warm affection that each knew would last as long as they lived.

12

THEY were just sitting down to dinner at Palmadora when Alma arrived.

"How perfectly wonderful to meet Leona's parents," she said joyously. "Funny; I meant to stay in Tampa a few days longer, but something seemed to urge me to come home. And when I think that if I hadn't, I might have missed you."

Lamar said with the usual twinkle in his eyes, "Oh, well, if you'd missed them on this trip, you'd have had another chance in about a month. They'll be coming back for Leona's wedding."

Alma put her spoon back beside the bowl of vichy-soisse and stared at Leona, wide-eyed.

"Leona's wedding?" she gasped. "Why doesn't somebody *tell* me about these things? How long has this been going on? And right under my nose, too!"

Lamar asked, "You don't even want to know whom she's going to marry?"

Alma recovered her spoon and put it into the soup, her eyes lowered to the task.

"Why should I have to ask? It's Cole Jordan, of course. Who else could it be?" she managed in a strained voice.

"Oh, Alma, *honestly!*" Leona protested. "It's not Cole Jordan at all."

Alma looked up at her sharply.

"Well, it had better not be Dr. Foster, or Paula will put arsenic in your face cream," she warned.

"Silly! It's Bruce, of course," Leona answered swiftly.

Alma's eyes widened slightly.

"Oh, boy, are you ever going to be in trouble!" she breathed softly. "Carol Decker will nail your hide to the barn door."

"Carol has already shot her bolt and is leaving Cypress Groves within a week," stated Lamar flatly, while Dr. Gregory and Irene listened in bewilderment.

"Alma," Leona leaned across the table, "do you know anything about what happened to Starlight?"

All hint of raillery left Alma's face, and she stared at Leona as though quite sure that Leona had lost her mind.

"You don't mean Carol had him destroyed?" she whispered after a moment.

"He just disappeared," Leona answered.

"Oh, but that's nonsense! He *couldn't!*" Alma protested.

"Sheriff Wilcox thinks he did. What's more, Carol accuses Leona of stealing the horse. She even swore out a warrant for Leona's arrest on the charge, and sent a wire to Leona's parents to come and rescue her."

Lamar spoke brusquely and to the point while Alma stared at him, so astounded that Leona knew Alma was completely innocent.

"Oh, boy, oh boy!" Alma murmured

at last in a tone of near stupefaction. "Leona, my child, if she did this to you *before* she knew you were engaged to Bruce, I shudder to think what she will do now that it's a sure thing you're going to marry him! Believe me, my girl, Cypress Groves, for all its hundreds and hundreds of acres, won't be big enough for both of you, and that's for sure!"

"It won't have to be," Lamar told her. "Rowley is serving an eviction notice on Carol and her mother, accompanied by a check I feel is far too generous. They are to be out of the Groves *and* the county by the end of next week."

"I can't help feeling a bit guilty about that," Leona admitted impulsively. "After all, Cypress Groves has been their home for a long time."

"Stop that nonsense," Lamar said sharply. "Uncle Dan left them a trust fund whose income is enough to make them moderately wealthy. And the check Bruce is giving them will make it possible for them to travel anywhere they want to, first class all the way. Carol can go husband-hunting anywhere in the world, and more power to her. If she was a rational girl, she would probably thank you for making all this possible."

"But since she's not rational by a million light years, I'd advise you to avoid dark alleys and secluded spots until she's out of the county," Alma said firmly.

"This Carol sounds like quite a character," observed Dr. Gregory. "Sounds as if she might be a prize patient for a psychiatrist. A *very* interesting study."

Alma nodded. "Very interesting indeed," she agreed, "for a psychiatrist. For just average normal everyday people, she's a very dangerous female."

Lamar said chidingly. "Now, Alma."

Alma cocked her head at him, her eyes narrowed.

"Now, Gramps!" she mimicked. "Don't tell me you're still falling for that wistful, limp-lily pose of hers, not after what she's tried to do to Leona."

Leona leaned toward Alma and asked

impulsively, "Alma, do *you* know where Starlight is?"

Alma stared at her, wide-eyed.

"Good grief, Leona, how could I?" she protested. "Oh, I get it. You're remembering what I said the day Bruce was hurt and you and I went out to keep dear, sweet, gently little Carol from having the horse shot. I told you coming back that if it became necessary, I'd steal the horse myself and hide him in Gramps' barn."

Lamar's bushy eyebrows went up. "Well, thanks a lot!"

"I didn't, though, Gramps, so don't get your feathers ruffled." Alma threw him a comforting grin. "Gramps, are you and Sheriff Wilcox sure that Sam doesn't know?"

"Quite sure," said Lamar, and his tone left no doubt that he *was* sure. "He's very distressed and upset and feels that he is to blame. Yet Wilcox and I both assured him that he wasn't expected to sleep in the stall with the horse. Starlight was there when Sam made his final rounds for the night; the horse wasn't there when feeding time came next morning."

"I hate to think what's going to happen to poor Bruce when he finds out," Alma sighed.

"Oh," said Leona gently, "he knows."

Alma stared at her, round-eyed.

"You told him?" she gasped.

Leona nodded. "I knew that most of the hospital personnel had heard rumors, and I was afraid he'd hear a garbled account, so I told him," she admitted.

"How did he take it?" asked Alma interestedly.

Leona's color rose.

"Oh, he was distressed, of course, but he didn't make too much of it," she admitted.

"I get it! You didn't tell him until *after* he knew you were in love with him," said Alma. "You couldn't have chosen a better time. To lose Starlight and find you— well, no man could ask for better luck."

"Do you mind, Alma?" asked Leona impulsively.

"Mind?" Alma's brows were drawn

together in a small, puzzled frown. "Mind what? Stop talking in riddles, angel. I've had a long hard drive, and the old brain isn't exactly functioning on all cylinders."

"Mind that Bruce wants to marry me."

Alma stared as if she thought Leona had lost her mind, and then suddenly she tilted back her head and her joyous laugh rang out.

"Oh, are you ever the blessed idjit!" Alma laughed. "Why, Lee, from the very first moment that Bruce saw you he's had it in mind. He didn't believe he could ever have the colossal luck, as he put it, to get you to care about him; but he was hooked from that first afternoon in Gramps' room. He gave me heck, after we'd gone, for making such a play for him in front of you. He wanted to get Carol off his back, but he was afraid you'd think he and I were serious about each other. It was you, not me!"

"I'm glad," said Leona, and beamed at Alma.

Alma studied her for a moment.

"Of course Bruce knew that you were

a dedicated nurse and your career meant a lot to you, so he wasn't sure he could persuade you to give it up. Are you going to?" she asked curiously.

"I'm going to do whatever Bruce wants me to do, always," said Leona.

"Oh, my sainted aunt!" Alma gasped. "Leona, don't ever let him hear you say that. Why, it will make your life miserable to be a docile li'l gal who just breathes by consent of her big, stalwart husband."

"It will do nothing of the kind," said Irene. "It will make for the happiest possible marriage. No husband worth his salt would take advantage of a wife who is genuinely anxious to do her part in a marriage. And you don't make a successful marriage by bickering about who's to be the boss."

"Oh?" Alma's eyes were wide and her tone was faintly touched with awe. "And to make a successful marriage, Mrs. Gregory, which one of the two *is* boss?"

Irene smiled tenderly at Amos, slipped

her hand in his and faced them with serenity.

"Neither, of course," she said gently, "Because in a successful marriage there's no necessity for a boss. It's partnership; an equal partnership; fifty-fifty all the way, in big decisions as well as little ones."

Alma nodded soberly. "Maybe I've been going at this marriage business all wrong," she admitted uneasily.

"I've tried to tell you that, but you wouldn't listen," Lamar reminded her.

"So you have, Gramps, so you have," Alma admitted, and once more looked at Irene hopefully. "I don't suppose you'd care to tell me how you hooked and landed Dr. Amos?"

Lamar and Dr. Amos looked affronted, but Irene laughed.

"I would not," she answered firmly, and smiled at Dr. Amos.

"She didn't," Dr. Amos said firmly. "I hooked and landed her. I took advantage of the fact that she was my patient and I made myself indispensable to her. And when I'd managed to convince her that we needed each other very much, I got her to a minister before she could change her mind."

"As if I ever could," Irene said softly.

Leona interrupted.

"I was the fly in the ointment that kept Irene from marrying Dad immediately," she stated flatly. "I was so jealous, so selfish, so hateful that I wonder Irene ever dared risk it. You see, I wanted Dad all to myself; and I didn't want Irene coming between us."

"Leona darling, this isn't necessary," pleaded Irene.

Leona smiled at her. "Oh, yes, it is. We've all been saying nasty things about Carol, and the more we find fault with Carol the more I can see some of my own faults. The only reason I came to Cypress City was because I was so jealous of Irene and Dad's happiness I couldn't bear to be in the same city with them. And then when I fell in love with Bruce, I suppose I sort of grew up. And high time, I'd say. I realized how much Irene and Dad meant to each other and saw what a rotten little dog in the manger I'd been. So now you know!"

She looked about the table, saw that Lamar and Alma looked a bit uncomfortable and smiled warmly at them.

"You are my dearest friends, and I wanted you to know the truth about me," she said quite honestly.

"Well, now that we do, we still like you. Don't we, Gramps?" said Alma.

"More than ever," Lamar answered, and his smile was warm and friendly.

"So, Alma, whatever Irene tells you about love and marriage, you listen, you hear me? She's an expert!"

"Oh, Leona, please! You embarrass me!" Irene protested.

Alma nodded thoughtfully.

"I'll listen," she said firmly. "And if ever I can get my man to the altar, I'll be the most docile little old wife you can imagine!"

"That," stated Gramps, "I would like to see."

For a moment all the gaiety and

warmth vanished from Alma's face and there was a darkness in her eyes that told of secret, unhappy thoughts.

"So would I, Gramps! So would I," she told him. And then as the dessert was brought in, she went on, "Now, this is mango ice cream and it's pretty special, so don't anybody dare to weep into it! We're all getting pretty teary, it seems to me. So watch it, folks."

13

THE next few days passed uneventfully. Bruce was recovering much faster than Dr. Foster had hoped and Dr. Foster unexpectly pleasant and friendly, had teasingly given Leona credit for that. Paula had offered friendly good wishes on the engagement, and the news that Carol and her mother had left Cypress Groves seemed to relieve Bruce even more.

"Mrs. Decker's a decent enough sort," Alma had told Leona casually, "but no match for that daughter of hers. You should have seen them drive away in a spanking new station wagon all gleaming with chromium, their belongings piled high, with Carol driving like Cleopatra on her barge going down the Nile."

She caught the flicker of expression on Leona's face and added sternly, "Now stop looking or feeling guilty, for Pete's sake! Gramps told you Bruce sent her a check that was far more generous than either the attorney or Gramps felt was required. Fifty thousand dollars! That, with the income from the trust fund Uncle Dan left them, will certainly keep them from begging in the streets, to say the least. I'd like to suggest the ranch-house at Cypress Groves be fumigated."

"Oh, Alma!" Leona protested, half-laughing but feeling a little less guilty at having deprived Carol and her mother of the home they had occupied for so long.

On the afternoon following the departure of the Deckers, Sam arrived at the hospital. He had been in several times to see Bruce during visitors' hours, but now he had an air of suppressed excitement that sent him rushing up the stairs and to Bruce's room in a hurry.

"I've got good news, Mr. Bruce, sir," he announced eagerly. "Starlight's back!"

"What!"

"True as true, Mr. Bruce." Sam's copper-skinned face was split with a white

240

grin and his dark eyes were eager. "He's in fine shape and looking like a million."

"But, Sam, where did you find him?" asked Bruce eagerly.

"That's the darnedest thing, Mr. Bruce. He was never lost. He'd been kidnapped. That fool Elbert had sneaked him out of the stable and over to his own place and turned him in with the tribe's herd," Sam reported.

Bruce, propped up against his pillows, could only stare at Sam, while his fingers reached for and found the bell-button cord above his bed. A moment later a PN appeared at the door and Bruce said quickly, "Ask Miss Gregory to come here, will you, Nurse? It's urgent."

"Of course, Mr. McClain," said the PN and glanced at Sam with a shy smile as she hurried away.

In a matter of moments Leona appeared in the doorway. She looked swiftly at Sam and then at Bruce as she hurried to the bedside.

"What is it, darling?" she asked anxiously.

"Tell her, Sam." Bruce's hand closed tightly on the one Leona had slipped unobtrusively to test his pulse.

"We've found Starlight, Miss Gregory," Sam reported happily.

"Oh, Sam! Is he all right?"

"Fit as a fiddle, Miss Gregory," Sam answered, "Elbert hid him in with the tribe's own herd. And of course when the sheriff came to search the stables at the Groves, Elbert wasn't there. And so soon as the Deckers were gone, and Elbert was sure they wouldn't be back, he came over riding Starlight and grinning from ear to ear. Mr. Bruce, you rarely see a Seminole smile when there are pale-faces around. But among ourselves we really have a lot of fun. Elbert was so tickled with himself for spiriting the horse away that I didn't have the heart to boot him off the place as I knew you would have wanted me to do."

"But why did he do it, Sam? And when he knew about the warrant for Miss Gregory's arrest, why didn't he come forward then?" demanded Bruce angrily.

Sam sobered. "Because he didn't think the danger to Starlight was over, Mr. Bruce. You see, Miss Carol had hired a couple of young men to steal the horse, shoot him and get rid of the body. She was fool enough not to realize that the men would go straight to Chief Charley and tell them the whole plot. Elbert sneaked the horse out; and the men pretended to Miss Decker they'd carried out her orders. So she swore out the warrant."

"Well, I'll be darned," said Bruce softly and his clasp of Leona's hand tightened. "Did you hear that, darling? I've got you; and now I've got Starlight again. How lucky can a man get?"

"And you're rid of the Deckers, Mr. Bruce," said Sam grimly. "I'd say that made you even more lucky."

Bruce nodded and drew a deep breath of relief and joy.

"Miss Gregory and I are going to be married, Sam, as soon as I can escape the hospital," he beamed at Sam. "So I really think a new day is about to start for Cypress Groves, don't you?"

"Oh, yes indeed, Mr. Bruce! I congratulate you both!" Sam answered happily. "And now I'd better be getting back to the ranch. What do you want me to do about Elbert?"

"Raise his salary," said Bruce firmly.

"Sam?" Leona asked as he turned to leave the room.

"Yes, Miss Gregory?"

"How did a Seminole ever get the name of 'Elbert'? I've been curious ever since I heard it," Leona admitted.

Sam chuckled. "Same way I got the name of Sam, Miss Gregory. Seminole names are difficult to pronounce, except by Seminoles; so in school and in later years, if we are lucky enough to go to college, we acquire 'pale-face' names for the convenience of teachers and others with whom we come in contact. Some of our names sound pretty crazy to pale-faces, which, by the way is a word we seldom use. Anyway, Elbert chose the name himself. He feels it gives him—what is that word?—prestige!"

Leona laughed, and Bruce joined her as Sam grinned and left the room.

"So now you have Starlight back." Leona spoke tenderly to Bruce as she adjusted his pillows and tucked the light covers about him.

"What's most important of all, I have you," Bruce told her. "I could have lived without Starlight and gradually have forgotten him, or even replaced him. But I couldn't live without you; I wouldn't even want to! You make it all seem worthwhile."

"Darling," said Leona softly, and bent to kiss him. . . .

It was a few days later, as Alma was leaving the hospital after her duty hours as a nurse's aide, that she met Dr. Jordan just outside the operating room

"Oh, hi," she greeted him breezily. "Busy tonight?"

"Well, no. Aren't you?" he answered cautiously.

"Oh, busy as a bee in a tar bucket,"

she assured him. "But we're short an extra man for a dinner party Gramps and I are giving, and I thought if you were free, you might like to trot out to Palmadora and join us."

"If there is anything I do enjoy, it's being invited at the last moment just to fill up a table," drawled Dr. Jordan.

"Well, it's your own fault," Alma pointed out. "If I'd had the faintest idea you were going to be free, I'd have asked you when the party was first planned. But I learned a long time ago that if I want to catch you free for an evening, I have to wait and pounce. So I'm pouncing. It's going to be broiled baby guinea hen and mango ice cream, and I know you would like them better than fried fish and canned peaches."

"You're appealing to my baser instincts." He grinned, amused at her airiness.

"Good! Delighted to know you have some! See you at seven!" She laughed and walked away.

He stood watching her until she had

vanished across the lobby and then, his handsome face taut and stern, he went on with his rounds.

It was a few minutes after seven when he drove up to the hacienda and parked. To his surprise, there were no other cars parked there, and he wondered as he walked toward the house if the other guests were even later than he.

As the front door opened before him, he greeted the butler pleasantly and then stopped as though a hand had been laid sharply on his shoulder. For Alma was coming toward him along the wide, cool hall, and she had never been more beautiful. She was always beautiful, he told himself even as his eyes swept over her in the floor-length picture gown of creamy taffeta with its delicately embroidered golden flowers that matched the golden-yellow orchid at her shoulder. Her hair was swept up and held in place with a wreath of orange blossoms, and as she came towards him, her lovely face was touched with a shy smile.

"Do you like it?" she asked demurely

as she revolved before him so that he could get the full effect of the beautiful gown.

"Very much." Dr. Jordan's voice was choked, so difficult was it for him not to tell her at once that she was a vision of devastating beauty. "Where are the others?"

A faint touch of pink crept into Alma's face, but her eyes met his innocently.

"The others?" she repeated as though she could not imagine what he meant.

"You did say a dinner party, didn't you?' he reminded her tautly.

"Did I?" Her brows went up as she dismissed the butler. When he had vanished, she answered Dr. Jordan quietly, "Well, how many does it take to make a party? I always thought two was sufficient. So did Gramps; that's why he's gone in town to dinner with Mr. Rowley."

For a long moment they stood quite still, their eyes meeting.What she saw in Dr. Jordan's eyes deepened the pink in Alma's cheeks.

248

"I thought we'd have dinner on the patio," she said with a surface gaiety that was not quite convincing as she led the way. "It's such a lovely night, don't you think?"

Dr. Jordan stood rigid for a moment, and then he followed her, tall and spectacularly handsome in his white dinner jacket, the dark red carnation adding a faint spicy scent to that of the orange blossoms in Alma's hair.

The table on the patio was wrought-iron, glass-topped. There were tall hurricane lamps lighting it, the candles glowing straight and tall within their etched crystal globes. Before them, the lawn was dew-wet velvet, with here and there a concealed floodlight hidden among the palms to illumine the scene and to make dancing ripples on the swimming pool.

Alma had regained her composure as they walked though the house to the patio, and now she turned and smiled gaily at Cole.

As he held her chair, Dr. Jordan looked

down at her uplifted face and asked quietly, "Why did you tell me it was a party, Alma?"

"Because it was the only way I could be sure to get you here, silly," said Alma cheerfully, and smiled as he walked around the table and seated himself. "We had Leona and her parents here recently, and I found you were on duty and couldn't leave. So I was determined you should come here as soon as possible."

When the butler had served their chilled consomme and had gone, Dr. Jordan locked his hands tightly on the table edge and leaned slightly toward her, his face white and set beneath its tan.

"Don't, Alma—*please* don't," he pleaded.

Alma stared at him, wide-eyed.

"Don't what, Cole?" she asked.

"Don't use me to whip this fool in Tampa into line," said Dr. Jordan harshly. "That's what you are doing, of course."

Alma caught her breath, and her eyes

were round with such shock and astonishment that Dr. Jordan was bewildered.

"You think I'm pursuing you just because I want to use you to get some nonexistent cretin to marry me?" she exploded so unexpectedly that he could only stare at her, scowling.

"Well, aren't you?" he asked and then caught his breath beneath the impact of a word she had used. *"Nonexistent?"*

"What else?" Alma demanded crossly. "It was you I was after all the time, only you were so snooty and hard to get. I've been after you ever since you first came to the hospital, but I tried not to bother you until you finished your internship."

"Well, then you may as well know," Dr. Jordan told her curtly: "you bothered me plenty from the very first!"

"I did?" Alma breathed eagerly.

"You did, indeed," he told her. "That's one of the reasons I broadcast my intention of becoming a luxury doctor. I thought if I did, there might just possibly be a chance for me with you. And then you started yapping about some guy in Tampa that you were trying to marry."

"I lied," she admitted. "It was you I was after all the time. I didn't dare try to use Bruce to whet your jealousy, if any! The poor guy would have been terrified. He was so busy running from Carol that I could have landed him just like *that*." She snapped her fingers. "Only I didn't want him. I wanted you."

He was watching her with a look that made her heart melt within her, and she held her breath, quite sure that he was going to thrust back his chair and come to take her into his arms. Instead, his jaw set hard and his eyes became bleak and cold.

"It wouldn't work, Alma," he said through his teeth.

She felt as though he had thrown his glass of ice water into her flushed face.

"Why wouldn't it, unless you don't care about me?" she whispered piteously at last.

"You know I'm crazily in love with you, Alma." He stated it so flatly that she blinked. "But just the same, it wouldn't work out."

"I can't see why not," she pleaded.

"That's because you don't want to," Dr. Jordan told her. "Look at it sanely, Alma. Here you are, born and bred to vast wealth and social prestige; here am I, a penniless nobody just about to graduate from a final year of internship and to be allowed to hang out my professional shingle and be free to starve for a few years until I build up a practice. Can't you see how impossible it would be if we were married?"

"I can't, because I love you, and to me, that's just about the most important thing in the world. How could a marriage work out unless two people were in love? If I were Leona Gregory, you'd marry me like a shot, wouldn't you?"

"No, because Leona Gregory is a charming girl, but she's not the girl I'm in love with."

"And I am?"

"You know that, darling."

"Then where's the problem?" she pleaded.

"You know that, too, Alma."

She drew a deep, hard breath and blinked away the mist that obscured her vision.

"You mean because of all this, of course," she said quietly, and her gesture took in the hacienda and the spreading acres of Palmadora. "Would you like to know that I'd cheerfully give up every single scrap of it and go eagerly to live with you in one room in Squatters' Row? I would, you know; only Gramps won't let me. I've got to keep Palmadora going after he's gone for the sake of the people who've lived and worked here for so many years. But does that mean I've got to give you up, just so that they can be sure of jobs and homes and schools for their children?"

"You're making it very hard for me, darling," he said huskily.

"I want to make it hard for you," she told him swiftly. "I want to make it so

254

hard for you that you'll see it my way. Please try, darling. Oh, *please* try!"

"Alma dearest, you'd have no respect for me if I came here to live and let you support me."

"Oh, fiddle-faddle, flap-doodle and nonsense," she exploded. "Look, do you suppose it's easy for me, you blessed *fool*, to wrap up what small bits of pride I have left and make a neat little bundle of them and lay 'em at your feet, begging you to marry me?"

"Alma, don't say that!"

"Well, it's true. I suppose it's because I've been brought up as a son of the family more than as a daughter," she said huskily. "I've had to make decisions, to give orders, to do a man's job. So I suppose when I fell in love, the only way I knew to go about getting the man I wanted was to pursue him. But I did hope that the man I loved would at least do me the courtesy of proposing and not make me do it all."

Her voice shook itself to silence, and she put both elbows on the table and hid her face behind her shaking hands while the butler, his copper-colored face as expressionless as one on a copper coin, removed the consomme and served the next course.

Dr. Jordan waited until the man had gone back into the house and then said very quietly, "I think I'd better go."

"Yes, I suppose you had." Alma managed to check the sob that tore at her throat. "And from this moment on, Dr. Jordan, I promise you faithfully you'll be perfectly safe from me. I'll never even glance your way again. And I'll stop being a nurse's aide. That way, we'll probably never meet again. And I'm sure you'll like that very much."

She pushed her chair back and got to her feet. Her heel caught in the long skirt and she stumbled. Dr. Jrdan was on his feet in time to steady her, and for a moment he stood holding her by the elbows. She tilted back her face, white now and with tears slipping down her cheeks. For a moment, in the steady light of the hurricane lamps, they stood thus;

256

and then Dr. Jordan caught his breath on a groan and she was in his arms.

For a long moment she clung to him, her tear-wet face hidden against his shoulder. And for all the rest of her life the spicy scent of carnations would bring back the memory of that poignant, heart-shaking moment.

She lifted her face at last, and as he would have bent his handsome head to kiss her, she put up her hand and laid it on his lips and drew herself free of his arms.

"No, Cole," she said huskily, "don't kiss me, unless you mean it for always. If I never know what your kisses are like, then I can't miss them, because you can't miss what you've never had."

"My dearest dear," his own voice was as husky, as shaken as hers, "more than anything else in the world I want to marry you. But I don't feel it would be fair to you."

She was standing away from him now, both shaking hands gripped hard on the wrought-iron back of the chair in which she had been sitting. The light of the hurricane candles showed him her face, tear-wet, white beneath its delicate golden tan.

"I suppose it *would* be fair for you to let me die an old maid?" she said. "Because that's what will happen. I never wanted to marry any man in my life until I met you; I know I'll never meet another I'd be willing to marry. But don't bother about me. You just go ahead and be noble, and I hope you'll be half as lonely as I'll be!"

For a moment they stood very still, watching each other. And then there was a faint softening of Dr. Jordan's sternly handsome face.

"*Mademoiselle,* would you do me the great honor of becoming my wife?" he asked then.

She caught her breath, and her slender body encased in the white-and-gold frock went rigid. Her eyes searched his desperately, and he waited, letting her gaze probe deep into his own.

"My dearest," he said very softly, "will you marry me?"

"Golly," Alma breathed childishly, her voice touched with awe. "Yes, of course I will. What else do you think I've been fighting for?"

Dr. Jordan's laugh was a caress as she came into his arms and her own went around him. Now she offered her kiss with a simple, unashamed ardor that he found very touching as well as very delightful. When the kiss had endured until neither could accept its ecstasy, she drew a little away from him and looked up at him anxiously.

"You really mean it? You won't change your mind?" she asked faintly.

Dr. Jordan laughed, a low, tender caressing laugh.

"Not if you'll promise never to be sorry you married a man whose income won't keep you in hair-do's," he told her.

"So I'll do my own hair." She broke off, unable to maintain her usual gaiety. "Oh, Cole, Cole, I've waited for this moment, and been so *scared* it wouldn't

259

ever happen. And now that it has I can scarcely believe it. You *did* ask me to marry you, didn't you?"

"You'd better bet that I did, my treasure." His arms drew her close again and held her tightly; his cheek pressed against her own. "I've wanted to for so long, and I didn't think I had a chance. First there was McClain, and then there was that guy in Tampa. I've been tempted to try to find out his name and then send him a neatly wrapped gift package of unpleasantly potent germs."

"And all the time he didn't even exist." Alma laughed and crept still closer in his arms.

The butler pushed open the door from the kitchen soundlessly, took one look at the scene before him and grinned as he went just as soundlessly back into the house.

14

THE news of the engagement of Alma Pruitt and Cole Jordan did not come as a complete surprise to the hospital staff. At least they insisted to each other that they had seen it coming. The surprise was the engagement of Leona and Bruce. Nobody, it seemed, had expected that.

"They're lying, of course," Jane Lester told Leona one day at lunch. "They're all saying, 'Well, of *course* we knew they were in love and were just wondering when they'd get around to announcing their engagement.' But they're lying. Not one of them so much as suspected it. For my part, I thought it would be Alma and Mr. McClain. And then you and he practically floored us."

Leona laughed joyously.

"It practically floored me, too," she admitted.

Jane chuckled. "I suppose it was the Decker girl's attack on you that brought the whole affair to a head, wasn't it?" she asked curiously.

"I suppose, in a way, it was," Leona agreed. "I'd offered my resignation and I'd gone up to say goodbye to him and—well, it just seemed to happen."

The two girls beamed at each other, and then Jane sighed wistfully.

"Two engagements in a single month," she mused. "It must be the scent of orange blossoms."

Leona laughed. "Well, they *are* pretty potent, at that."

"Funny," said Jane, and shook her head sadly. "They haven't affected me that way, and I've been here three years!"

"Well, don't lose hope," Leona teased her lightly. "One of these days a handsome young millionaire may crash his car near here, and you'll be assigned to nurse him, and who knows what may happen?"

"Ha!" Jane derided her. "He wouldn't have to be handsome *or* a millionaire, just as long as he was under fifty and unmarried."

The pretty Seminole waitress came with their dessert. When she had gone Jane asked, "Will you be leaving the hospital after you're married, Leona?"

"I suppose so," Leona answered. "Bruce and I haven't discussed it. I'll do whatever he wants me to do, of course."

"Well, of course," Jane agreed as if there could not possibly be any other decision. "I suppose we'll be getting a new surgical nurse then. I only hope she'll be as nice as you, Leona. I'm going to miss you."

"Thanks, honey; you're sweet. But I'll only be a few miles away, and I'll want you to come out when you're free. Who knows? Maybe Bruce and I can find that under fifty, unmarried man for you," Leona laughed.

"I'll take you up on that, don't think I won't!" Jane threatened.

Leona looked about the dining room. There were all her friends now: the other RN's, the practical nurses, the interns, and staff. She would miss them all, as well as the busy routine of the hospital. And yet might not her routine as Bruce's wife be equally busy and even more rewarding?

"Don't look so smug." Jane's admonition reached through Leona's absorption. "I'm trying hard not to hate you, but if you keep on looking like the cat that has just polished off the family canary, I won't be responsible for my emotions."

Leona laughed and patted Jane's hand. "I didn't mean to be smug," she apologized. "It's just that I'm so happy I can't help it."

"Sure," Jane forgave her. "And I'm that pleased for you! But I guess we'd both better get back to work. There are people here who aren't as happy and hearty as we are, poor souls."

"Sit down, Jordan." Dr. Foster motioned to the chair across from his own where he sat behind his desk. "Cigarette?"

"Thanks." Dr. Jordan accepted it.

"I don't think I've had the opportunity

to congratulate you on your good fortune in respect to Alma. She's a wonderful girl and you're a very lucky man."

"I realize that fully," Dr. Jordan admitted, and waited cautiously. What the devil, he could not help but wonder was on Dr. F's mind?

"I'm sure you do," Dr. Foster said. "I don't suppose you've had any chance to make plans for your immediate future, after you're through here at the hospital? Private practice, I suppose?"

Dr. Jordan hesitated for a moment. "That was my original plan," he said. "But now I'm wondering if Cypress City really needs another doctor freshly fledged and just starting up in business."

"You hadn't planned to stay in Cypress City?"

"Well, not until Alma and I got engaged," Dr. Jordan replied. "But Mr. Pruitt seems to feel that she cannot be spared from Palmadora, so I suppose we'll have to stay. That's as far as any of my plans have gone, and you can see how vague they are."

Dr. Foster nodded. "I can," he agreed. "I was wondering how you would feel about staying on at the hospital as my chief assistant."

Dr. Jordan's handsome face hardened slightly, and there was a look of uneasiness in his eyes as Dr. Foster went on.

"I'm sure I don't have to tell you how heavy the pressure on me has been for the past several years. I've had my eye out for someone I felt I could trust; someone who is a skilled and capable surgeon and who has something I seem to lack: a proper 'bedside manner'." He grinned wryly. "You seem to have a way with the patients, and you qualify in every other respect. So if you'd care to stay on, I'd be happy to have you."

There was a moment of tense silence, and then Dr. Jordan put the thought in his mind into words.

"I suppose Lamar Pruitt is behind this offer?"

Dr. Foster scowled.

"And may I ask why you should think

Mr. Pruitt had anything to do with my offer?" asked Dr. Foster harshly.

Dr. Jordan's mouth was thin-lipped and hard.

"It was a perfectly natural conclusion, Doctor," he said dryly. "I've been here for quite a while, and never until my engagement to Miss Pruitt have you so much as hinted you would like me to stay."

"Not until your engagement to Miss Pruitt did I have any idea that you intended to stay on at Cypress City," Dr. Foster said. "I took it for granted that when you'd finished with your surgical internship, you'd be off to some large city to practice your profession. When I found you and Miss Pruitt were going to be married, I felt sure Mr. Pruitt would not want her to leave Palmadora. She's been brought up from babyhood to assume responsibilities there; trained to take over after he is gone. But I am afraid I resent your suggestion that Mr. Pruitt has offered to subsidize your stay here by arranging to have you permanently engaged here at the hospital. That *was* what you meant, I take it?"

"What else could I mean?" Dr. Jordan answered, and there was a grimness in his tone that matched the look in his eyes.

"Well, you can get that idea out of your head immediately," said Dr. Foster curtly. "You surely realize how under-staffed and overworked we are here, how badly an assistant in surgery is needed. You're doing a fine job, Jordan, and I wouldn't hesitate for a moment to turn over to you the most complicated operation."

"Thanks, that's very kind of you," said Dr. Jordan.

"It's not at all," Dr. Foster objected. "It's simply the truth. And if it will aid you in making your decision, perhaps I should add that we are going to ease the workload for everybody shortly. We have three new interns coming in at the end of the month. They are Cuban refugees, men who have worked in Havana hospitals and who have had refresher courses here in Florida; men who have been carefully screened by the FBI, and who have won high grades in the State Medical Board examinations. With the ones we already have, and with a new surgical nurse to replace Miss Gregory, the workload should be considerably less by mid-summer."

Dr. Jordan was listening intently, and when Dr. Foster paused, he said quietly, "Your offer is very flattering, Doctor, and I'll be happy to accept."

"Splendid." Dr. Foster was obviously very pleased. He picked up his telephone and asked the girl at the switchboard, "If Miss Ingram is in her office, will you please ask her to step in here for a moment?"

He replaced the telephone and addressed Dr. Jordan again.

"We'll discuss the question of money later, Dr. Jordan, if you don't mind. It's almost time for morning rounds, and I'd like to show you the books, get an accounting from the bookkeeping department and let you see just what you're getting into. Will that be satisfactory?"

The door opened to admit Paula, smartly coiffed, immaculately uniformed, her smile cool and professional.

"Oh, come in, Paula." Dr. Foster rose to greet her. "I have some good news. Dr. Jordan is not leaving us. In fact, he's joining the staff as my chief assistant in surgery."

Paula's smile deepened.

"I'm delighted, Cole," she said. "Dr. Foster desperately needs you, and since you are familiar with the hospital, I know you are going to be a vast help to him and to all of us."

"Thanks, I'll try to be," Dr. Jordan answered, and felt a trifle dazed at the unexpected warmth and friendliness of both these people in whom he had seen very little of either emotion in the past.

"I'm sure you will be." Paula smiled at him and took up the telephone as it clamored on Dr. Foster's desk. "Miss Ingram."

"Oh, thanks. I'll take the call in my office, Reba." As she replaced the telephone she said to Dr. Foster, "The

Nurses' Registry in Jacksonville. I'm trying to find a replacement for Miss Gregory."

As she reached the door, she paused to say lightly, "I wish we could offer *her* a proposition that would persuade her to stay. But I suppose that would be impossible. It's different with women. What's that old corny phrase, 'Love is of man's life a thing apart; 'tis woman's whole existence'."

For just a moment she looked straight at Dr. Foster, and in her eyes there was a tenderness that was very nearly a caress. And then she was gone, but Dr. Foster still looked at the door that had closed behind her. And Dr. Jordan asked himself curiously, Do you suppose he's such a dumb cluck that he's just discovering she's in love with him? The whole hospital has known it for years!

"Well, guess we'd better get at those rounds, Doctor," said Dr. Foster, and they walked together out of the office.

Dr. Jordan was just finishing his rounds when Alma arrived.

"Hello, precious," she greeted him softly. "Our date for tonight is off, darn it."

Dr. Jordan kissed her lingeringly and asked with polite surprise, "Oh, did we have a date for tonight?"

"You hound!" Alma protested. "Of course we did. But Gramps has suddenly taken it into his head that he wants to attend a cattle auction in Kississimee, and of course he can't drive. And besides, he says he wants me to help him decide. Which is just downright silly, because there's a magnificent Brahma bull that's going on the block, and Gramps is going to have fits if he doesn't get him. He's already made up his mind. The beast will go for at least fifteen thousand dollars, and Gramps thinks he can blame me for being extravagant provided I'm along and agree to the purchase."

"If," said Dr. Jordan gently, his eyes brimming with tender amusement, "you will close that lovely mouth of yours for a minute, I have some news for you; a surprise. That is, I *hope* it's a surprise."

"I love surprises. Tell me quick," Alma urged.

"I'm staying on at the hospital as Dr. Foster's chief assistant," Dr. Jordan told her.

She stared at him for a moment, and then she gave a small, bubbling laugh. "And I'm supposed to be surprised?"

"Well, aren't you?"

"Golly, why should I be?" Alma pointed out. "Dr. Foster's smart, and he needs a chief assistant, and you're the best man he'll ever have, so why shouldn't he want you?"

Dr. Jordan's hands were on her arms now, holding her a little away from him.

"This isn't something you and your precious Gramps cooked up?" he demanded.

Alma's eyes rounded in astonishment.

"Why, you *dope!*" she exploded, and wrenched herself free of him. "Do you think Gramps would try to *buy* me a husband, or that I'd let him, if he did?"

"Well, I just wondered—" Dr. Jordan began.

"Then you can stop wondering, you so-and-so," she flashed at him. "Gramps would never meddle in my affairs; and my marriage is most definitely my affair. It would never occur to him. Cole, I'm trying very hard not to be awfully angry with you. But if this is the way you are going to react to every good thing that happens to you, then maybe we'd better call our marriage off right here and now."

"I'm sorry, darling."

"And you should be," Alma flashed at him. Then suddenly tears filled her eyes and her lovely face crumpled. "Oh, darling, I didn't ask to be born a Pruitt and a girl. I didn't ask to be trained to run the place when Gramps is gone. I have been penalized all my life because I was rich and the owner of Palmadora. I did think, I hoped against hope, that you wouldn't hold it against me. I can't help it, Cole. Don't you see that? It's not my fault I have to live there and keep things going; or that you have to live there with me and maybe give up a brilliant career; I'd go anywhere in the world with you, darling, and consider it pure joy, except that I can't let Gramps down when he's counting on me."

She was in Dr. Jordan's arms long before she had finished, weeping against his shoulder, and he was holding her closely and murmuring loving, tender words into her ear.

"Forgive me, dearest?" he murmured against her ear.

"Always," she told him with a deeply touching simplicity, and suddenly gave a small laugh. "And I was the one who told Leona she shouldn't be a docile, willing little bride, saying, "Yes, darling," to her husband and always doing as she was told. And now—why, I'm always going to walk humbly two paces in the rear."

Dr. Jordan stopped her words with an ardent kiss, and after that neither of them seemed to feel any further words were necessary. For them both the hospital corridor was suddenly flooded with golden sunlight, and Alma was quite sure she heard a chorus of angels singing joyously.

"My dearest dear," said Dr. Jordan at last.

"Yes, darling?"

"I love you."

"Oh, thank you, darling! And I love you, too, so much it almost hurts! Oh, Cole dearest, we are going to be so happy, aren't we?" she breathed, her cheek against his, her lips touching his ear.

"So happy," he answered tenderly, "that they'll probably charge us a tax on it."

"And we'll pay it and think it's the world's most superlative bargain." She chuckled softly and tried the impossible: to creep even closer into his arms, which were already holding her so close she could scarcely breathe. Fortunately, it made it that much easier for his mouth to reach hers in a lingering kiss.

Other titles in the
Linford Romance Library:

ROMANCE AT REDWAYS
Jane Lester

Darbie Ferris had been born with an insatiable itch to put things right for those people who were not as happy as she was. Kenward Marr, the new RSO at Redways, could have told her that people don't always want to be "fixed", but Darbie had to learn everything the hard way.

NURSE DOYLE IN DANGER
Jill Murray

Heartache threatens Nurse Thelma Doyle when the ex-girlfriend of RSO Gavin Yeomans returns to the hospital as a very sick patient. She is under the delusion that she is still engaged to Gavin, and, as she is so ill, Gavin goes along with this. Thelma does not see the danger signals until it is almost too late . . .

THIEF
OF
MY HEART
Mary Raymond

Olivia met Nicholas Sherburne and his family in Paris and he deliberately sought her out when they returned to London, for she was just the girl he wanted to look after his nephew while the child's parents were away. The arrangement suited everybody—except Nicholas's sister-in-law . . .

THE
WILD MAN
Margaret Rome

Curupira—the wild man! No wonder, thought Rebel, the primitive natives of the Amazon used that name for Luiz Manchete. She had never met anyone quite like him. But Rebel soon realised that his only love was, and always would be, the Amazon . . .

NEW DOCTOR AT NORTHMOOR
by Anne Durham

Doctor Mark Bayfield had managed to get on the wrong side of every member of the Kinglake family. But when young Gwenny Kinglake went into the hospital, Doctor Bayfield was the only man who was likely to diagnose the problem.

THE ENEMY WITHIN
by Nan Herbert

Marian undertakes to care for her young niece, but as she has also accepted a post as a Surgery Nurse, her fiancé, Hugh, protests, since Marian will have less time for him. When she receives an offensive anonymous letter, Marian suspects that Hugh might have written it!

REBEL IN LOVE
by Lilian Peake

Lex Moran, a man of considerable power, decided that the local school was uneconomic and should be closed down. But Katrine, the schoolteacher, felt passionately that the school should be saved, and she was determined to oppose Lex in every possible way.

NIGHT NURSE AT NASSINGHAM'S
by Quenna Tilbury

Christine Thorby was expected to become engaged to Dr. Peter Temscott, but the engagement never took place and Peter went to another hospital. It looked as though the same thing would happen when Martin Redway, the Surgical Registrar, fell in love with Christine . . .

DR. SIMON'S SECRET
by Kathleen Treves

Deborah Markham had just arrived to start her nursing training at Sappington General Hospital when she met Langdale Simon. Met him and fell in love, little knowing that he was the R.M.O. at the hospital where she would be working. But she was soon to find that loving Doctor Simon was not an easy matter . . .

LOVE FROM LINDA
by Kay Winchester

Nurse Linda Brooke, has no premonition of the impact on her life when three casualties arrive at the hospital late one night. They are Aurelle Boulton; a lorry driver with a shady past; and famous racing driver Cedric Deacon.